ULTRA HEAVY

ULTRA HEAVY

Book 1: Edge of Empire

Tim Kirby

Multipolar Press
2026

ULTRA HEAVY

© 2026 Multipolar Press

First edition

Published by Multipolar Press

multipolarpress.com

ISBN: 978-1-970784-10-7

Edited by Constantin von Hoffmeister

Contents

Chapter 0: A Statement from the Tsar

If You are reading this, then it means that I am dead and that You most likely killed Me. Thus, the Throne with all of its terrible responsibility is now Yours. As Our glorious history dictates, even the greatest of leaders leave life with one titanic failure looming on the horizon—the lack of a worthy heir. If You are seeing these words within the midst and mist in Your mind, that means that You are that worthy heir. Either You defeated Me after senility consumed everything left of My being, or You were selected rightly from among the crowd of potent candidates by Me just before passing through death's doorstep to meet Our Creator.

My dear Heir, our new Tsar, I wish You a long life and many successes! I both congratulate and pity You, for You have a long and brutal road ahead, carrying on Your shoulders by far the heaviest cross to bear of any human being in the solar system. Every day of Your reign, You will hear the cries of millions who assume in their hearts that You can solve their every problem with the simple wave of a scepter. They think that We are God made flesh, who can do anything instantly if We merely will it to be so.

But… although We may seem omnipotent compared to Our mortal citizens toiling in the fields and factories, We, with all Our might, are but ants compared to the glory of God Himself. The greatest sin of any leader is to overstep his bounds and foolishly declare himself a living god. This is the one sin of a Tsar that is truly unforgivable.

Ours is to fight evil and keep the 3,000 years of Russian history continuing on as far into the future as We can as the Katechon. This is Our Prime Directive. Nothing more than this can be done. Only God can create utopia. We can only beg Him for mercy and abide by His rules to achieve salvation in death, living in a flawed and sinful world.

This information that has been directly uploaded to Your consciousness is everything that You need to know to rule. We should start Your indoctrination to the Throne with a story that few if any know of besides Myself. It transpired not that long ago and is very telling about the nature of Our people, Our ideals and Your duty as the emperor of Our great civilization.

I have provided notes and redactions where I believe clarification or omission is necessary. Be aware that this historical account was compiled under My direct authority, meaning, it is from My perspective, as those directly involved did not leave a formal account of what transpired. But I shall tell You this: the Throne under My direct order monitored these events with great interest and I tell You that they are *pravda* as a whole, but *istina* at their core.

Since this information is directly in Your mind, it is hard to say if there is a formal beginning or end to it. These forms of uploaded data ultimately become amorphous within Our skulls. But I can say, and should repeat, that We have begun Your indoctrination to rule from the Throne with a story of one man who lost faith in Our eternal ideals. He lost faith in everything, and, more so than anything, he lost the will to live. The greatest moment of heroism is not triumph but that of utter despair, when a man rises to reject his misery, when he decides to take bold action regardless of the cost, when he stands to meet his destiny head-on.

This is a tale of heroism, great deeds, and the philosophy behind Our empire of 3,000 years in all of its many iterations.

Go with God, and do not take the decision to extend

Your life for centuries lightly. This choice has many "drawbacks."

Chapter 1: The Last Straw

Thud, thud, thud, the noise of his heavy frame plodding against the metal staircase resounded off the rusting walls. Every ligament burned and twisted as he made his way down each bent step. After three centuries of being shot, burnt and blown up, only to be regenerated… piece by piece… time and again… age and consequences had begun to set in. He held the railing of the metal staircase like a pensioner leaving a train station. Hunching over, he could feel every impact of bone and metal within his legs sending a burning fire of pain up his spinal cord. His massive weight, which provided unmatched combat potential in the past, had become like a yoke around his neck in the present.

Through his golden-bronze, battered helm, he spoke to himself in dire frustration. "Why, why do they never listen? These young idiots never know when to wait. They never understand when to negotiate. The passions of youth consume them, every, damn, time."

The staircase of metal led down into a hazy subterranean world underneath the vehicle factory. This production line was the first one of its kind set up on Mars, a key achievement of our progress into assimilating the Solar System and another example of the brilliant execution of the Prime Directive by Tsars past. Who knows how many millions of civilian vehicles rolled off this assembly line in all sorts of configurations and colors. Each of our colonies, and Mother Russia itself back on Earth, are expansive and without proper transport our people would live helpless lives as the prisoners of its vastness. In her day, this factory was a beauty, but alas, the Curse of Terraforming, and neglect, ultimately took the workers of this beautiful institution from us, and thus our hero and many of our brave young soldiers from his Domain were sent in.

From the purple-grey smoky heights, our warrior shambled downwards into an orange and red haze. Around him, he could see wires, tubes, racks, pipes—all the organs of a living industrial and economic system that had recently gone dead. The fiery light from below pulsed over the edges of all these mechanical innards.

[Note from the Tsar: Our man had been sent to deal with a factory uprising. These happen from time to time and you should be aware of this. God has given man free will, and we as Tsar should respect this, but we cannot let foolish passions get in the way of the economy. But, this my Heir, was no normal uprising. It became quite clear that the Curse had taken hold viciously here. Needless to say, upon seeing the abominations, the young men from the Domain of our hero simply chose to open fire without being ordered to do so and with no particular strategy other than to avoid death. Young minds panic first, especially when dealing with the Curse's abominations.]

Finally coming to level ground on a landing, the pain in his knees could return to its usual dull background level. He saw a few bodies lying around. He quietly crept towards them to get a better look. They were humanoid and non-uniformed. Their exteriors looked to be of a white glossy material rather than skin. But their insides, which had become partially "outsides" from rifle fire, were quite normal and had a burgundy red appearance. It was almost like someone had dropped human-shaped eggs on the floor—white and brittle on the outside, and viscous on the interior, cracking into chunks upon impact.

Our hero continued to move forward holding his 12.7 mm heavy machine gun in firing position with one hand bracing it under his armpit and holding onto the railing with the other. Continuing his agonizing descent into the glowing underbelly of the factory, he could not wait to get this all over with. He had had enough of this repetitive profession of his.

He reached another landing. This one was far broader and was probably the place where they could maintain the actual assembly line machinery from below. It was a maintenance zone of sorts. As he slowly moved through the area, he passed the dead body of the third son of the couple who lived on lot #7 within his Domain. His first beard had only just started to grow in. The young man's life had only just begun and yet it was already over—a story of one chapter with no time for a plot to have developed.

He winced on the inside, sighed deeply in despair and thought to himself, *Again... again... I'll have to look another mother in the eye and tell her, her son is dead... again they died on my watch... again because I'm too old and too slow to lead from the front... again!... again!*

The helm linked directly to his mind and allowed him to scan the dead youth through various spectrums and in every direction. The data came quickly and he felt a sense of pure disgust. The wounds on the fallen teenager were under his chin and armpit.

He cried out silently within his own mind, *This idiot has a full suit of armor on... and yet... he didn't maintain his posture! The moron! The idiot! He died because he didn't have faith in his chest plate and shoulder pads... he just fell over in fear and got shot from below. He exposed his belly to the lion's claws! Christ save me! He exposed all the gaps... his own fear killed him. This is what they tell you on day one in the army: never let them shoot at you from below; always keep your plates tight, no gaps! Why didn't they just wait for my old ass to go in first!? Why didn't they just wait? This dead body should have been me!*

He wanted to plead out loud to God at the top of his

voice in frustration. He wanted to scream at this young man till he came back to life, but now was not the time to make noise. Normally, his helm offered "omniscient" vision, giving a full view of everything around him with multiple different filters for thermal, infrared and so on. But the hot steam and thick metal walls were blocking nearly all of the signal strength. His prophetic cybernetic vision was reduced to a few meters in all directions, making it basically worthless.

In a way, he was going into this tomb of horrors blind, but it was clear that at least something was moving down there and that it was definitely warm-blooded—no machines this time.

He made his way down further through tunnels and corridors, all below the great machinery of the historic automotive plant. He came to a vast open room that seemed to have been of great importance centuries ago. Through the grates and gaps of the production line above, glowing red and orange lights cast rays down on him and everything around. Where he stood looked to be something like the interior of a submarine or sewage system, only far more vast. Vents, pipes, wires, all laid with purpose seemed very chaotic to one who did not know their specific purpose. But on the floor of this chamber he saw a horrible sight.

Upon the metal beneath his feet lay untold numbers of bodies, mostly the pure white beings that had been turned into shattered teacups coated in red stains. But alas, all the men he had brought with him also lay dead, overwhelmed by far greater numbers, their dark armor showing dozens of successfully saved impacts, and yet it was not enough. "Quantity has a quality all of its own," as Joseph Stalin is believed to have said.

He investigated the bodies further with his physical eyes and kept the back of his mind looking in 360° for any surprises. The problem for him was, with his legs throbbing in agony, how could he possibly spin around to face a threat from the rear like in the good ole days? Within seconds, without his proper omniscient vision from his helm, he could be attacked from anywhere. Keeping in mind that his youth was far behind him and that he had many limitations at present, he stepped backwards to keep his spine to the wall, thereby reducing all possible angles of attack. Above him was solid material and not grating, below his feet many millimeters of rusting classical steel. For the moment he could only be shot at from 180° via a horizontal angle of attack. But with all his men dead, now what would he do? Did the abominations escape, or perhaps they were all already dead?

"My good man, I offer you an olive branch of friendship." These words rang out as if sung by a choir coming from seemingly nowhere. They echoed off the hard, rusting surfaces of the factory, its industrial environment projected the vibrating words like a cathedral. "There is much to discuss, my new friend. There is no need to continue this aggression. There is no need for violence against a potential ally." The voice, or so to say cluster of voices, was both male and female; it was both synchronous and yet chaotic. On pure instinct, still blinded by the metal walls and steaming mists, our hero turned to the sound holding his machine gun with both hands, poised to fire like the statues that adorn my... or should I say... your Kremlin.

From the darkness emerged a large porcelain-white being, four meters tall, surrounded by like-colored but averaged sized "men." It moved like a dancer in the Caucasus mountains, seeming to float with perfect grace across the body-ridden floor. The creature's fluidity of movement was unparalleled. Its flowing blonde hair followed along through the air as if it were underwater. And, it was unclear if it was clothed or if it was merely shaped like a woman wearing a formal gown. Was it flesh, cloth or something else? Its otherworldly growing bright aura made it hard to determine just what our hero was actually looking at.

He could see its bleach-white underlings were armed and they were not that many in number. The boys from his Domain must have killed a lot of them before he arrived. Among them though, there were two with anti-tank rockets. No matter what the case, be they mutants, machines, marauders, or monsters, somehow at least one of them always got their hands on the good stuff, the kind of weapons that could end the suffering of our hero in one shot. He knew he could survive nearly any exchange of rifle fire, but rockets hit hard and they always found the gaps. They could blow through even the best *troika* steel given a direct hit. Thus, they would be the priority. He noted in his mind, *Check targets, rocket #1, rocket #2,* and his helm began to provide continuous targeting data, which was somewhat superfluous given the distance and bothersome steaming mist.

"I sense your, fear my brother. I know that the weaponry of some of my children perturb you..." As the entity spoke those words, its forces began to point their guns up towards the ceiling in unison in a seeming gesture of peace. "You are right to fear the rockets; you are after all... only human."

Our warrior was stunned. Of all the mutants, freaks, and abominations of mankind that he had seen, surely nothing could read his thoughts that directly. The being looked much like a statue of a Roman god in a flowing toga of sorts. Its flesh was of the finest porcelain and yet it moved with the flexibility of normal meat and sinew. Its hair was of a slightly blonde tint and continued floating as if in zero gravity while it spoke. The entity exuded a soft golden glow, seemingly coming from within it—a form of bioluminescence. The chorus of a single voice began to continue.

"My brother, I know your pain, the pain you live with every day. You've lived the life of a hero; you've lived the lifetimes of many warriors in length, but soon you are fated to be an invalid. Your body is becoming a coffin for your mind. Trust me, my dearest friend, I know this to be true. No amount of nanorestoration can turn back the clock. How many times do you think you can regrow your body before it finally gives out? You cannot do this forever and you know it!"

Our warrior kept silent, controlling his thoughts, trying to shift to pure combat instinct and "turn his mind off." He stood poised with his gun perfectly trained on the face of the tea-cup-skinned entity.

"You may try as hard as you like to hide your thoughts, but there is no need to fear me. There is no need to kill me, my dear brother. I am no threat to you. In fact, quite the opposite, I am the solution you have been praying for. I have the answer to your paradoxical condition within me. I am your salvation!"

The fighter in armor sensed that he was being "backed into a corner" and needed to shift the dialogue to a sustainable position. He barked forth a bold declaration, "I, on behalf of the Tsar, in all His greatness, offer you the chance to come home, lay down your arms and I assure you none shall be punished. Our great empire seeks harmony and stability. Disarm, end your uprising, stop trying to read my thoughts, and we will work out how to proceed equitably within the framework of Holy Rus'."

The entity placed its hand over its heart as if it were an offended princess. "Brother, why do you lie to me? You know your offer is empty. Your solution does not solve your problem; my solution does. You pray to God every night to take you in your sleep, in battle, in an accident. All you ask is to die a hero and yet your God denies you. He laughs at your misery from the cross. My blood, my kin, all you want is to have your suffering end, to never wind up in a wheelchair staring out the window having forgotten everything you fought for. Soon you won't even be able to stand, yet your brain could carry on for generations to come. You could rot away like a vegetable for decades, no, centuries! You do not want to slowly rust away, trapped for untold years in a lifeless body, or even worse, having to be put down like a dog by your battle brothers. You fear your own kind will come for you, soldier of the empire! You fear that one of the young ones will come and crush your skull under his boot, a final humiliation to annul your lifetime of heroism! You cannot lie to me; I know you better than you know yourself!"

The entity was right on all accounts. It spread its arms like an old woman pleading to her grandchildren, adding theatrics to its monologue.

"My solution to you is this: if you merge with me, if we become one, I will get your endless strength, but you will get my eternal youth. Together we shall live in a state of rapture, more powerful than the Tsar, greater than all the monstrosities of the Fascists, more potent than a million Southerners. We will be greater! Both of us will get our heart's desire!"

Our warrior could see on the huge porcelain entity many faces swirling on its glistening skin. He could only surmise that it was type of organic collective consciousness. It would seem that it had absorbed the best and brightest at the factory and turned the remaining workers into thralls for manual labor and as a meat shield. This creature has impressive strategic reasoning despite it being a manifestation of Satan. Its oratory and psychic skills were certainly… palpable. Our hero fell silent. Unmoving, unspeaking, he maintained his posture. His mind began to swirl with the words of the freakish cluster of creatures. Was it speaking in words from without or was it already inside of his brain and speaking from within? He could no longer tell.

The harmony of voices bellowed out with some frustrated indignation, "My brother, you again lie to yourself in your mind. We can be unstoppable; you can be a hero again. Merge with me; give me your strength. You will never fade away… and we together… shall… become a god!"

And within one-sixtieth of one second, he activated his internal converter to maximum and his finger pulled the trigger.

The look of forced theatrical concern for his fellow man on the porcelain god's face was shattered by the first bullet smashing through the bridge of its nose. Cracks of rupturing ceramic spread throughout its head. The bolt of the machine gun went back slamming forward to put another round in the chamber. Holding the trigger down, the second bullet exploding forward driving through and fully toppling out of the back of its skull spinning like a contact football after a punt. Another round was ripped from the belt and slammed into the chamber; the previous round's casing was ejected with unearthly grace dancing through the air. The third shot went forth and caused its head to completely explode into gallons of scarlet goo with blood spraying from its neck as if it had been pressurized. The geyser of gore sprayed the grated ceiling.

He directed the next explosions from his barrel as the remaining thralls quickly started poising their weapons to fire as our hero adjusted his aim. Thanks to his various cybernetic modifications, there were few if anyone who could take the initiative against one of the greatest of Holy Rus'. For him, a brief few seconds were often plenty to work with.

Doogh, doogh, doogh, the machine gun belched with bass as the muzzle flair ignited the room with the light of righteousness. Porcelain body parts flew through the air like butterflies in summer as the fire continued. He swung the barrel of his gun, maintaining fire onto the first rocket specialist of the mutant horde. One round hit it in the leg, blowing it clean off. It fell forward, only for a second round to go through the top of its skull, sending vertebrae flying like shrapnel in all directions.

He swung the barrel towards where the other rocket launcher was at, letting rounds rip as he moved blasting through the poorly armed monstrosities.But as with age, he was just ever so slightly too slow. By the time he put the first round through the icy-skinned thrall's chest, the rocket was well on its way.

He "felt" the launch through his helm, and our hero, in that brief moment, could see the projected flight path. He pushed off with his left leg to get his body moving to the right, to get out of its path and far from the wall, but in that moment, he felt a snap. His knee buckled under the weight of his body and the years of degenerative nanorestoration. The ligaments couldn't hold up his quarter-ton frame trying to move with explosive force. He started to fall face forward. His internal converter was blazing away, making these single tenths of seconds seem to him like an eternity, and yet still he could not react in time.

All he could think was, *Not again, oh God Almighty not again, please take me to your Kingdom!*

Sensing the warhead, anti-rocket flak burst from a front panels on his Hauberk automatically. The shreds of metal hit the explosive device at about two meters' distance. Kneeling like a broken prisoner, or better yet like those who faced the executioner's blade, he met the warhead's wrath. It exploded away, shredding through any possible gaps in his armor.

His lifeless body blasted by the explosion hit the ground, his helm registering dozens of impacts, many penetrating across weak points in his suit of armor. As he went down, by pure instinct alone, he maintained fire where he thought the remnants of the mutant mob were standing. Bleeding, deafened and nearly blinded, he kept shooting from prone. Mutant after mutant met their grisly end from the horrific power of the 12.7 mm rounds. His helm continued to function until the bitter end.

With an empty click, his belt of ammo ran out.

The passage under the factory floor fell silent.

All bodies were lifeless.

Our hero lay in a pool of gore without movement. Inside his helm off to the side of his mind, a message was displayed. It said: "6.5 hours of nanorestoration to regain functionality."

Unable to move, staring blankly forward, he could see his left gauntlet. On it was written: "Ultra Heavy #148"—the only name he had had and the only meaning that had been for his life for the last 300 years. But was any of this worth it? What was the point of these three centuries? Did being blown up over and over again actually accomplish something? How much longer could he keep doing this? How many more men would he lead to their grave while he would live on? Questions in his mind only led to more questions.

Lying lifeless among the dead, feeling the nanomachines race around to restore metal and flesh, he had time to contemplate, and to face the reality that the porcelain god was right: his life was over; he was faced with rotting away trapped in an ever-restoring but decaying body. He was doomed to become an invalid unable to fulfill his duty to God, his civilization and to Us, the Tsars. Existence was no longer a blessing, but a curse.

Something in his life had to change. Something had to be done. He couldn't go on like this anymore.

Chapter 2: An Audience with the Tsar

Ultra Heavy #148 sat upon a cold stone bench staring directly downwards, his head unmoving within his golden-bronze helm. The halls of the Kremlin were designed to be both impressive and oppressive, the perfect message for a waiting area to send. It reflected the greatness of our abilities, and thus sent a clear message, "Don't waste our time with trivial affairs."Massive statues of heroes past towered over the mortals in the endless hall from above. The dark green marble of the walls and hidden warm-colored lighting made those waiting feel as if they were in line for something significant, something extraordinary. The red glow from behind the green stone provided a brutal yet elegant otherworldly atmosphere in the finest tradition of imperial architecture.

[Note from the Tsar: My Heir, you should never forget the importance that architecture plays in human psychology— no one can believe that they live in a glorious empire if the architecture around them shows the opposite message to the public daily. Any expense for powerful and ideological architecture is always worth any cost. Would you believe in the Glory of the Kingdom of God if He resided in a shed instead of a church?]

The dark green fabric covering his armor glowed at the edges with hints of the warm indirect light as if he was a burning ember. It glinted off his semi-polished helm, dancing like the thoughts in his mind. And, indeed, his consciousness was ablaze in reasoning. Any audience with the Tsar, even for a man of such importance, was a "one-shot" and sometimes "once-in-a-lifetime" attempt to pitch an idea or file a complaint directly with the emperor himself.

Every five or ten minutes, armed guards would politely ask each person waiting in line to move one marble bench closer to their eventual goal: a private audience with Us the Tsar. #148 could read on the faces of those leaving the Throne room whether they got the answer they had wanted or not. The populace always naively thinks that the empire has infinite resources and it is merely a matter of asking "the Big Boss" to get any problem solved. They are absolutely sure that every wrong can be righted by complaining incoherently to power, but this has never been and never will be the case. It is the duty of the Tsar to make our Civilization survive into the future as the Katechon, not to play the role of Grandfather Frost granting wishes for the adult-child masses. But in the end, hearing these audiences from the people creates stability, for their voices are heard, directly by Us, even if their ideas, or should I say demands and wishful thinking, are unfeasible and often completely insane.

[Note from the Tsar: It is critical that we maintain the opportunity for the public to have an audience with Us regardless of the quality of the results of such interactions. Although 95% of the complaints they issue are utter trivial nonsense, the other 5% is of dire importance. Once or twice per session of audiences, I hear of an issue or two that We would never be otherwise aware of and that needs to be dealt with. It is worth the aggravation of hearing bored elderly women complain about the noise of teenagers in order for a few "gems" to be found within the muck. I highly suggest and implore You to maintain this policy

throughout your reign.]

A young guard of the Throne sharply approached our hero. "Respected citizen, please forgive my rudeness but I do not know how to address you. Your first name being '148' must be an error of some sort? I mean to say that…" Our man cut him off, "It's no mistake." A few awkward seconds passed… "Please forgive me, but how can I allow a 'number' to visit the ruler of our Holy Empire?" After taking in a deep breath, he replied with cold sarcasm, "Stop talking to me and ask Him yourself; he'll set the record straight."

The young Kremlin guard looked terrified. The gears in his head were grinding as to whether it would be better for his career to question the documentation slowing the day's audiences to a halt or allow some unknown entity to speak to the Tsar himself. Both options seemed like potential career enders.

He looked into the externally reddish visor upon the helm of #148, gazing at his impressive set of armor with serial numbers matching his "name" to his passport. Time seemed to take an eternity as he perused this giant man leaning his elbow on one knee, partially hunched over like a mob boss on the cold stone bench right before the entrance to the Throne room. "Respected citizen, number One Hundred and Forty-Eight, you have been granted one hour… wow one whole hour!?... of the Tsar's time for a private audience, please proceed through the golden doors."

[Note from the Tsar: At the time of writing, only a little over 1,200 Ultra Heavies were forged, but many of them were already dead, and even fewer sought an audience with their "Employer," thus the guard's confusion. The Inner Guard need to be elite to keep the Tsar in good health; the Outer Guard is fine for ignorant but loyal teenagers.

Furthermore, being referred to by number of entrance

into the status of Ultra Heavy seemed like a good idea at the time. I myself thought it would be powerful to see a passport with just a number on it. It was to be a rebaptism of sorts into a new status. This move would protect one's family and personal relationships through total anonymity on all documents, completely deleting one's past. Sadly, this move has merely led to bureaucratic dissonance. This is one mistake of my rule that You would be wise to correct by some means.]

Slowly standing up, his torn ligaments and battered bones, regrown yet again from his last outing at the Martian car factory, crunched and squeaked within his body. To sit down was pleasure; to stand up was pain. He limped forward and through the massive gold-plated doors into the darkness, armed this time only with his wits.

As he entered, he saw the heavily equipped Inner Guard and various secretaries in high heels and miniskirts quickly leaving the Throne room. This was an "off-the-record" meeting after all, and no one could harm the Tsar without some very heavy weaponry, not even an Ultra Heavy. The Inner Guard were for more ceremonial and aesthetic purposes. Then again, their gear looked clean and impressive. The four guards sized up #148 as they walked past him like dogs from a different pack. One of the secretaries gently turned her head and gave a princess-like wave of greeting to him as she trotted away awkwardly in platform high heels. They locked eyes through his visor, but he chose not to react to any of these minor players. He had bigger goals in mind.

As #148 approached, I saw one of our greatest heroes, hobbling, broken, and old. I could see there was a glint of life in him as he perused my secretaries as they left, but that was animal instinct. Despite his many triumphs, just from his gait I could see he found that father time was defeating him. When you have the biometric data of every citizen directly linked to your mind, the age of 333 years stands out as impressive and ancient but perhaps broken and senile as well. I wasn't quite sure what to expect from the oldest remaining Ultra Heavy.

He moved to the center of the Throne room slowly and fell to one knee as is tradition. His weight made a booming thud as his armor and frame within it hit the marble and metal of the floor with a slam.

Despite the massive size of the Ultra Heavy, he was dwarfed by the architecture of the Throne room. Around the circular chamber were statues of all the events of the 3,000 years of our history with some room to spare for the next millennium. Alexander Nevsky, Ivan IV, Ivan Ilyin, Joseph Stalin and many others looked down with a glaringly negative expression on their faces. It looked as if all of them would come to life and say to their progeny, "You owe us". The figures were of dark bronze and the floor was the same material with patches of marble for elegance. The room was kept purposely dim as to give a sense of mystery. Aesthetics are important!

And thus I spoke, "Ultra Heavy #148... I wasn't expecting a man of your caliber among the bickering old ladies today... I am glad to see you are still alive... and in service." "Thank you for your warm greetings, Sir," he replied quickly, more out of trained reaction than thoughtfulness.

A few long seconds of time clicked away in silence.

Someone needed to break the stalemate of nothingness and so I started, "Well... you requested a private audience... what is it that you have to say? This is off the record... so tell me like it is... without the formalities, that is to say... don't bullshit me, what's the problem?" Sadly, our hero came near the end of the day when my patience was already paper thin.

[Note from the Tsar: You should take into account that

since many fear you, they will respect you, but they will always want to tell you what they think you want to hear. This is one of the curses of sitting on the Throne—an unending river of fake news filled to the brim with bubbling white lies from well-meaning yes-men. Our citizens speak Pravdoo when formal, but speak only Istinoo in their kitchen or in the locker room, thus I changed the tone of the conversation accordingly to "guy talk." This is a good rhetorical strategy for most men.]

#148 slowly took off his helm and revealed the scarred face and pale grey eyes of a man who had seen many lifetimes worth of dark days. He rubbed his gauntleted hand through his short grey hair. "Boss, I am grateful to You, I am grateful to Holy Rus'; I love my job; I have no regrets." "But," I replied sharply. He continued promptly, "But, my knees have been damaged and regrown so many times… that… I can barely walk… Sir, I can't do my job and I am lucky to make it to the toilet on time at this point." I didn't like where this was going and bluntly replied, "Perhaps this conversation should be on the record. I can't remember one of my men having the balls to make a defecation joke to the Tsar!" He looked into the blank sockets of my metallic skull, knowing he did something wrong and yet continued somehow unabated. "Look, Boss, this needs to end, I've got nothing left."

Now I was starting to get angry because of the disrespect, musings of dereliction of duty, and disorganized thoughts, all from one of our "finest." Something here didn't add up. "You know that there are millions of our people who'd give anything to live for hundreds of years like you do, to heal wounds as if Christ's hand touched them. You've been blessed with top-tier cybernetics and nanomachines not for your own fun and personal pleasure, but for public service. The only reason your knees have grown back is to get your ass back out there and keep the empire the fuck afloat. You got me, boy?"

#148 raised his hands to plead… But I needed to drive the point home. "How many smoking hot 20-year-old wives have you had the chance to have after 300 years? How many sons bear your legacy? Don't you have domain over 1,000 hectares of good flat Martian soil? When was the last time you even thought about money? The only way you get out from under that armor is by death, and if you even think about suicide… the greatest sin in the eyes of God… then I'll kill you personally right here and now to make sure you go to the Kingdom of Heaven directly."

When a 4-meter-tall, metallic, armored, cybernetic skeleton chews you out, even Ultra Heavies back down… sometimes.

"No, no, sir, I'm not asking to go into retirement. I know that there is no relenting one's duty… and that God forbids suicide…the Church is clear on this… Ultra Heavy is a status that cannot be undone. I should know. I am the one who 'retired' #5 after dementia ate his brain from the inside… what I mean is that…"

I leaned back on my throne out of curiosity and interrupted his rebuttal. "#5? He was quite a dashing man in his youth. I knew him well. He was very good with the ladies with the hair and all." #148 could only shrug confused by the change of direction in the conversation. "By the time I put the mace through his skull, he had no hair left, nor the mind to be aware of that fact, or smooth-talk women." Deeply saddened, I sighed in my own way at the thought of this long-lost memory. He truly was a dashing hero, the kind that represented something greater than himself. That man truly loved life.

"Look… Boss… I am the opposite of #5. His brain rotted out, but his body was still fit for combat. His fate was clear and sealed. I am lining up to be a mentally fit invalid, a working mind trapped in a rotted out all-too-mortal shell. I know I can't quit, and I am not going to live in a body that is rusting shut."

"Yes, and?" I said, motioning my hand for him to push this along.

"I formally request from you, Tsar of Holy Rus', in all your wisdom, for a mission from which I will never return."

A few seconds of contemplation were required.

"Boss, give me a way out, I beg you. I've got nothing left."

Three more long seconds passed in silence as I considered his words…

"You wish to challenge fate? Bold. You shall get what you desire. You have my word," I said clearly and resolutely. This proposal actually worked out very well timing wise as You will see. Interestingly, #148 remained silent. He stared at Me waiting for the next move to come from my voice box. I "left the locker room" and returned to my more formal imperial tone.

"There is one particularly brutal issue that needs to be dealt with and yet has virtually no chance of success. It would seem to be the mission of your dreams. #148, you are probably aware that we have finally gone beyond Jupiter for the first time and we have successfully terraformed Titan. The public was informed that we started this insanely difficult and expensive project, but due to the risks of failure and the Curse, we didn't let it be well known that we had already sent colonists to Titan. The moon has definitely been terraformed, but 'can anyone actually survive there?' is an entirely different question.

It is within the realm of normalcy for distant colonies to maintain contact poorly during their first phases of development. There are solar flares, bad planetary alignment, malfeasance from our solar-system-wide geopolitical adversaries and so on. But this time, it looks like we may have lost the whole damn thing. For the last few weeks, we've needed someone with… very little to lose… to volunteer to go there and send data back on what happened at minimum and at maximum solve or kill the problem.

We cannot allow the Curse to take hold at this tentative stage. The occasional mutant uprising on a stable planet is fine, but a total clean-slate mutation of all the colonists… if that happened… will have grave implications for the future of Saturnian development. And Titan is the very last location that we can definitely terraform. All other prospects look bleak at this point. It is our last hope for expansion."

#148 seemed to ponder my words. He raised his eyebrows and exhaled almost in relief. "I can send back a signal; I can slaughter another hundred mutants; I can die on Titan for You, my Lord; I can do anything as long as my service to You and the State ends."

"Looks like we have a deal, I'll miss you, #148. You've done a hell of a job over the last three centuries. Shame about failing nanorestoration and all." He replied with a strange tone, "Nothing lasts forever, Sir." I replied with a mystic tone, "But things can be prolonged indefinitely, and that's why we need Titan." Our hero did not understand what I was hinting at. At times, I have to make inside jokes for my own amusement to maintain my sanity.

And with that, he donned his helm, stood back up on shaking knees and shambled away back into the darkness from whence he came.

He walked back down the waiting hall slowly and in silence, passing a middle-aged blonde woman sitting on the final bench before the Tsar where #148 had just been. Her eyes fixated on the floor, her hands shaking with nerves. The golden ornate *kokoshnik* on her head cast a shadow over half of her face, exposing only her fragile tiny chin to the light. Her glistening hair was tied in a single braid running down her back. The lass's tight body was covered in form-fitting ceremonial-class armor from neck to toe.

High heels and other embellishments of the female form were part of the design, even while sitting her stomach looked flat as a board. Her legs were crossed tightly like a knot. Judging by the lady's grim expression and trembling, she had something very dire to tell Me indeed. The state of dismay and peril she exuded blocked the shine of her fading beauty.

Chapter 3: Heavy Landing

And thus, #148 slept as he was sent beyond Jupiter protected from the effects of radiation and zero-gravity degeneration. We have made great progress in space travel and yet it still requires days or weeks to move over the extreme distances of our empire. This significant trip to him would seem like only a moment as he hurled through space at speeds incomprehensible on land. He was the only "crewman" aboard a one-way small transport ship of nearly minimum size. By his request, instead of perhaps brave volunteers, he chose to take vast amounts of meal rations and weapons. These lay around him, filling the ship to the brim with green boxy containers placed and secured in perfect order. The Curse never seems to affect absolutely everyone at a given location, meaning that a militia could and should be rallied to resist whatever evil lurked on that moon of Saturn. Our hero would surely find some living allies from the remnants of the colony, right? Militias are fed by food and ammo and he took with him quite a banquet.

[Note from the Tsar: Although the Curse causes Us great problems, killing thousands every year on all of Our non-Earth territories, there is nothing that unites Our people like a good existential threat. Fighting for the survival of our Holy Empire with rifle and bayonet changes male citizens for the better. They become forged with a deeper meaning that merely existence for the sake of existence cannot provide alone. The common man may see side effects of terraforming as a 'Curse' but it is a bizarre twisted blessing of sorts when you really think about it. I fear the

day when we've terraformed everything terraformable, and when we finally break the Curse. At that moment, we will encounter the deadliest of threat to all of humanity: meaninglessness. Now that You are in power, my Heir, I beg you to keep in mind that if there is nothing to fight for, if there is not struggle to existence, no glorious goal on the horizon, no God, nothing sacred, then that is when humanity's flame will go out forever. Always find something new for our people to die for or everything our ancestors died for will be in vain. I tell you now and will repeat to You that your burden is ultra heavy.]

After quite some time, the ship entered the thick glowing atmosphere of Titan. The flight path was correct and the AI whirred with zeroes and ones, calculating the proper trajectory to land near the site of where the colony should be. The ship rocked and shook in a terrifying way but there was no one conscious to experience it. Bursting through the clouds, the craft was exposed to a world mostly barren. Over purple-stained rocks and dirt grew the first sparse trees the planet had ever known. As it got closer and closer, fields of thin grass appeared and the ship's camera clicked away with delight, taking as many images as it could from this high vantage point. Releasing the parachutes, the craft began its final descent, now facing vertically upwards like a dolphin at play.

The ship touched down and gently bowed forwards, and came to a final rest in the proper position: horizontal.

Some time passed and our hero began to come to his senses.

Opening his eyes, he was greeted with data from his helm floating in his mind:

- Landing successful
- Ship Damage: 1%
- Fuel Remaining: 7%

- Battery Status: 51%
- External Air Quality: acceptable
- Humanoid Life Within 500m: none detected
- Additional Environmental Threats: none detected
- Open Airlocks? Yes/No

"Sure, why not?" he replied verbally.

The system finished its message to his helm:

Crew Status: 11 of 12 dead. Is this an emergency?

"Considering I'm alone, the math looks right on this one. There is no emergency, computer."

The lid to his protective chamber calmly began to open. Dim yellow daylight filled the matte grey metallic interior of the ship. #148 sat up… or at least he tried to. Sleeping in uniform, he was quite crammed into the pod designed for a common citizen. He tried again to sit up… and failed. *I hate getting old,* he thought to himself. He rolled his right shoulder downwards in order to get sideways. He pushed himself up with a closed fist on his right arm only to realize that his knees were stuck in that position. They had nowhere to bend and, considering they barely worked at all, this strategy wouldn't do. Lying back down, he used his free hand to force his leg upwards. This time the push worked and he got onto one knee like a contact football player resting on the sideline. He pushed down on his knee with his arms while pulling himself up. Quietly he spoke to himself, "If it took that much effort just to get out of bed, I think the colony I was sent here to save is probably fucked."

As he was consumed with shame for his aging feebleness, his eyes were drawn to the horizon though the small window at the front of the ship. Even after more than a thousand years of space travel, the human mind cannot tolerate living in a space with no windows, no view to the outside. Windows have to be built even for trips where 95% of the journey would be spent unconscious. Humanity never changes… well except for the Fascists.

Through the thick yet narrow glass, he saw a vast and open landscape under a soupy dense sky. It was hard to tell what time of day it was as the Saturnian moons are so distant that only a thick atmosphere sitting atop an Earth-like lower layer could trap enough sunlight for positive temperatures. That muddy layered sky is a technological achievement of cataclysmic 3D chemistry thought impossible during our predecessors' time. Jupiter's moons were hard enough to terraform and demanded insane effort, but no one thought that we could get enough heat to start converting Saturn's largest moon. True, Titan was lush with organic compounds and nitrogen, making the job, in some ways, vastly easier than its peers. But, maintaining a climate above zero degrees this far from the Sun is a testament to the glory of God and our Holy Empire. Yet again we have done what others deemed undoable. The impossible has occurred. Any of our citizens should enjoy a nearly permanent "October in Moscow" on the surface of Titan near the equator. They shall not freeze, but nor shall they swim for any extended period of time.

Below the orange porridge sky and in more normal tones of color lie barren rolling hills, a tiny spattering of young trees, probably the first generation to grow, with thin grass and moss surviving wherever water could pool. To #148 the planet looked like a house under construction: the walls, roof, and window were in place, but it was not ready for people to move in. It had great potential but it was far too desolate. There was not nearly enough biomatter to feed into converters for a colony of hundreds of thousands of citizens. *Perhaps the colony has gone silent simply due to a lack of fuel?* he thought to himself. *Maybe it is just that simple; they sent the ship prematurely… bad math leading to hundreds of slow, suffering deaths.*

Turning around, he saw that the ship was packed to the brim with cargo, guns, ammo, and canned food. Everything was done as per his request. All of these goods were packed away in cargo containers strapped to the floor. And most importantly, there were a few travel-sized converters, each bright brilliant and cubic as they were always produced. They looked to be something like a small freezer opening from the top and made of metal painted white. These ones were military-grade, and thus could take a few major "dings" before going out of service. There isn't that much organic matter here to convert but there was enough... probably. If he was completely alone on the planet, then there would certainly be enough. Then again, he had no time to spend countless hours gathering organics. He decided not to risk it by putting all his eggs in one basket.

"Computer, deploy solar panels," he said in a clear commanding tone. The ship's AI confirmed the order and began opening some exterior shielding. The display on the control panel displayed the following:

- Solar Panel Shields Lowered
- Operational Capacity 100%
- Light Levels: Minimal
- Total Expected Energy Output per Day: 0.2 kWh

"Yeah, only organic material is going to cut it... feces, rotting food, dead bodies, anything to get some decent gasoline," he said to himself. The sky was simply too soupy, the sun simply too far. Perhaps this was even the brightest day of the year and things would only get darker? This would not be enough energy to heat the ship at night, keep the AI running, turn the lights on and do whatever else requiring electricity. Well, while there was still energy in the battery he decided to get all the info out of the AI that he could.

"Computer, present the data you recorded upon entry

into the atmosphere, especially topographical and thermal mapping. I need all scans of every spectrum uploaded directly to my helm." The computer understood the request and began to send blurry maps and pock-marked data to his head armor. Looking at the new map in his mind, he could see this planet had very few sources of heat. There was very little that stood out from the ambient temperature. One would expect even just one ship for colonization to yield a few small settlements but there was virtually nothing. One large signature and two smaller signatures overall. He thought to himself with great ponder, *One of these three would definitely be the colony ship itself, if it was operational. Perhaps the other two locations are spread out far from it for the sake of farming? There should be just enough plant life to maintain livestock.*

So, every heat source and probably every sentient being on this planet is packed neatly into this triangle? Something isn't right here, that's not how primary settlement is done. There should be some buildings, organized streets, but this is just a mess, completely structureless, but why? he thought to himself. *The smaller two dots of heat were much closer, but how could anyone survive out here with such little energy usage? They'd be living like cavemen, or has it taken over something that doesn't exude heat?*

"Computer, in the photographs that you took during entry, did you detect any artificial structures, vehicles or human presence?" Three seconds passed and the answer displayed boldly on the screen: "*Nyet.*"

He touched his gauntlet to the sensor on the control pad. "Computer, review the files from my gauntlet drive. Tell me, was there anything about this primary colonization mission that was any different from, say, Mars or Ganymede?"

The screen glowed with the single word: "Analyzing," and a progress bar slowly growing at the bottom. A warning popped up: "This operation requires significant energy output to complete. Do you wish to continue?". "Yes," he said out loud and immediately.

#148 began to again look out the front window and across the horizon. He could feel the wilderness calling for him to go out but he needed to know what he was getting into. Tactics without an overall strategy always spelled doom. The progress bar got to full after what seemed like an eternity. The computer began to type out a response: "The primary colonization of Titan differs from previous imperial experiences in post-terraforming colonization in the following ways:

- The preparations and loading of the ship along with crew selections were done in 5 weeks and not the standard 6 months.
- No follow up secondary or tertiary ships were launched after receiving the 'green light' from the successful landing of the first ship.
- No data of any kind regarding the success or failure of the new colony was received by the Throne.

In every other way, shape and form, besides those listed above, this colonization ship and its mission line up with the tendencies and best practices of other successful attempts.

Some classified information has been omitted. Was this answer helpful? Would you like to know more about Titan or inter-systemic transport ships?"

He looked down at the end of the information and made another request, "Computer, please explain what you mean by 'classified information has been omitted'?"

The AI grinded for a moment, then provided another written answer: "This data includes Throne-level secured information. Are you completely alone to view this panel, Ultra Heavy #148?"

"Yes, I am completely alone," he replied coldly to the machine mind.

The ship's systems began to write their answer: "These

are the words of the Tsar Himself, praise His wisdom and may He live long on the Throne! Message start: The colonization of Titan is presumed to have failed for unknown reasons. No one has even a clue as to why. There is zero information at hand. This is the only completely failed primary colonization attempt in the history of Our Holy Rus'. It is Our one and only grand failure in this regard, and cannot be acknowledged to the public until we find an acceptable 'bandage' to put over the wound. We are currently searching for the right kind of crew with 'nothing to lose' to throw at Titan to at least get basic information as to what went wrong. These men are sure to die, but the information they gather could save hundreds of lives and provide a bright imperial future on Titan. For reasons too humiliating to Holy Rus', I cannot disclose the reasons why the second and third colony ships did not launch. But I can say that God has blessed Us with this 'failure' as their crews would surely be doomed and their numbers were far greater than that of the first vessel. I can only assume that there are hundreds of corpses rotting there now. We shall not throw thousands more human beings into the beaker of this terraforming experiment. Information must be attained in order to determine what shall be done about this national embarrassment. Message end."

#148 thought to himself slowly letting the gears of his mind churn for a bit... *For being a planet of hundreds of dead men, there's certainly some heat being generated. After this amount of time, there is no way this is just automated machines or farm animals or some natural phenomenon. Someone out there is alive, but why with all the ship's communications devices they couldn't send a signal to Moscow makes no sense... or... perhaps there are forces making sure that no one sends any signals back home?*

He could feel a structure of understanding starting to build in his mind. Colonists were still alive somewhere, and the complete lack of communication with the Throne must have been on purpose. At the very least he could confirm that the ship didn't crash. In that event, the planet would be devoid of any heat signatures at all.

"Computer, relay all the topographical and thermal data back to the Tsar's Throne. Include a transcript of everything we have said to each other thus far."

The computer wrote on its display panel:

- Request understood.
- Data package gathered.
- Data package being sent.
- Time till receipt: Over one hour.

"Good," he said out loud and shifted over towards the long cargo crate nearest his travel pod. Being that it was designed for use by one of the Empire's finest, it was adorned with quotes from great men of great ages, and Biblical prayers. Most prominently displayed was Corinthians 5:21:

> *"God made him who had no sin to be sin*
> *for us, so that in him we might become the*
> *righteousness of God."*

All men need reminders that greatness surrounds them even when completely alone on a potentially dying planet. He groaned as he went down to a knee to open it, flipping its latches upwards for what could be the very last time.

He opened the lid to see his primary weapon: his perso*nal Dyuzhina* 12.7 mm infantry heavy machine gun. It was tough, reliable, old, battle-damaged, and antiquated— just like its operator. The dark metal, with countless bright glinting scratches and dents felt oh so familiar. It had been customized to be comfortable to be used without a tripod. The ergonomics were perfect and oh so familiar to him. He took out one of the packaged ammunition belts, put in the first round, slammed down the hood and charged the first round with a resounding "clack" bouncing off the metal walls of the vessel. Although he was at the threshold of the end of his life, there were few things as beautiful as that sound. One should take the time to appreciate the simple beauty that surrounds us and nothing sounded better than the first round harshly going into the chamber.

Unlike his gun, he had chewed through a lot of maces over the years. Every Ultra Heavy carries a melee weapon, mostly for good propaganda imagery. Standing triumphant over a fallen foe holding cold steel makes for better monuments and movie posters. Obviously, there can come times in close quarters, a lack of ammo, or facing a unique foe, that the Ultra Heavies can flex their mechanically enhanced muscle directly. Although a one-handed sword of various shapes and sizes is certainly a classic option, maces in the right hands can cause incredible internal damage without needing to penetrate armor. An Ultra Heavy armed with a mace can simply bash in the biological or mechanical brains of an enemy without the need to pierce any armor. This provided great combat flexibility and reliability.

#148 lifted his newest and what he presumed to be his final mace. A standard-length, blackened, carbon-hardened *troika* steel truncheon with a spiked cylindrical shaped head at the end. His number was etched onto the shaft and next to it a prayer: "Lord Jesus Christ, have mercy on me." The sacred words from some 4,000 years ago were as blunt yet effective as the mace itself. #148 smiled to himself, amused by this irony.

There was also a pistol even more disposable than any mace he wielded and a set of grenades designed for dealing with "crowd control."

All geared up, he again asked the ship's computer to run diagnostics on the external air quality and pressure as well as radiation levels. Although he did feel slightly "lighter" on Titan, the AI assured him that the gravity was the only thing noticeably different than Earth, with a dissonance of

5%. That and the overall dimness of the sky during midday seemed to be the only key differences.

With a gush of air, the seal of the ship was broken. The boarding plank, made of metal many centimeters thick, slowly lowered. Tipping up his helm, our man gently sniffed the air just to see if the AI had let him down.

Glory to God, glory to the Tsar, it's perfect, he thought to himself. He disabled the filtration systems in the helm as there was no need for them. He breathed air as clean as on a mountaintop all the way back on Earth. It was a bit thin but excellent and crisp. Flexing the muscles of his mind, he coordinated the data the ship gathered with what his visor was able to detect. He had a clear path ahead of himself to the first minor heat signature. He had all the food and weapons he'd need to survive for years. Now all he had to do is find out if there were any other humans still alive on this world besides himself.

He waved his gauntlet over the boarding plank to lock up the ship. If he wasn't alone, there was no need to put a small army's worth of guns into the wrong hands.

Looking out, he could see pale blue at the horizon, fading up into a canary yellow and eventually a rusty orange cloud belt at the top of the heavens. A few valleys lay ahead. It was time to march into the unknown, hopefully, for our hero, for the very last time.

Chapter 4: The Locals

Negotiating was mentally tough, but physically easy. Fighting was mentally easy, but physically tough, but walking after 300 years in armor was grinding his mind and body as the kilometers passed. Everywhere there was a rock to make his knee go the wrong way or black oil leaking from the surface, perfect for bringing down an aging titan on Titan. And then a gentle rain began to patter against his helm and pauldrons as he wearily continued on.

Suddenly he came up to a small ledge and he saw something moving in the distance. He took a scan of it to see its heat signature. It was definitely hot and definitely biological. He moved just a few quick steps to get closer and saw them… a herd of cows deep in the distance. They were chewing and staring off at the horizon as bovines do.

He moved smoothly but cautiously towards the cluster of cows. They looked to be in excellent health but slightly lean, eating what little grass there was to eject "fuel" later. There is no way a domesticated pack of animals could survive with every human dead. There must be "shepherds" to oversee the herd, but where are they? Or are these cows alone surviving on instinctual auto-pilot?

Suddenly he heard the gallop of hooves and sensed motion coming from behind him. "Ah, there they are," he said quietly. He stood ready with the noble posture one has after walking away from countless impossible fights. The riders approached, each atop a dark horse and wearing what looked to be dark blue plastic tarps over themselves like hooded capes. Only their bearded chins stuck out from under the plastic cowls. #148 scanned them with his helm.

They were surely humanoid in shape. They had a few minor tools with them and that's it, no weapons, nothing of a technological level beyond the early Industrial Revolution. *Something isn't right,* he thought to himself.

The riders pulled back the reins, forcing their horses to stop. "Who the fuck are you?" the man in the middle demanded to know. #148 raised his hand to mid-chest to provide the answer. "Is 'fuck you' really the best way to start off a conversation? Look, I don't want your cows. I just want information," he stated calmly and confidently. The middle horseman took a few long seconds to reply, "Well... then... where the fuck did you come from? Is that better?" The men on horseback chuckled at the witty sarcasm. In an equally sarcastic tone, he gave a response, "Well, see, when you ask in a more respectful way, I am much more motivated to answer... I have come on behalf of the Tsar, from Moscow proper. I represent his will and the will of the people of Holy Rus', which I can only assume... includes you fine sirs."

The horsemen seemed to almost recoil in quiet shock. "But the Tsar is dead. There ain't no more Russia. It's over man." #148 seemed just as surprised as the plastic-wrapped cowboys. "I can assure you, at least the brain of the Tsar is very much alive and he is quite the conversationalist..." One of the riders interrupted, "But, if the Tsar is alive, then, why did you abandon us here, why'd you leave us to die?"

This was quite the informational attack that he would need to quickly and convincingly parry.

"Wait! No one abandoned you. My presence is testament to that fact! I don't know why it has taken so long to send another ship to Titan, but I am here now and I need to know what is going on so we can get this planet colonized properly," he said calmly but very firmly.

"If that's true, then why are you alone?... If what you're saying is true, shouldn't there be dozens of you, and new colony ships?... Now, I see you've got a real nice gun on your back, but how is that going to help us build a better life here? What are you gonna do? Shoot us into fucking prosperity?" His colleagues snickered at the sarcasm.

"The gun isn't a plan or strategy. I don't have a plan because I have zero information. As of a few minutes ago, I can only now confirm that some of the original colonists… and their cows… are alive. All the Tsar told me is that this colony had gone quiet."

"It went 'quiet' years ago, man. Is there something wrong with the Boss's bolts? Because it sure took him a long ass time to notice the 'silence,' homie."

"Look, my countrymen, I can only apologize on behalf of the Tsar and his Throne for the lack of action on our side. Yes, you probably feel abandoned here; perhaps you feel betrayed, but I am here to find a way to fix things… if they need fixing… I'm on your side… But first, tell me, in your opinion, why this expensive, fairly large, well equipped colony has gone completely offline?"

The three cowboys looked at each other, not really sure how to respond, or if they should really stick their neck out by revealing the truth.

[Note from the Tsar: My Heir, one thing is for sure: whenever anything doesn't work out, no matter what our approval rating is, they'll always blame the Tsar. This is a reality that You will have to live with: "You can't please all of the people all of the time."]

It is hard to say what was going through the minds of the men on horseback, but they had been forced into a Mexican standoff of who would answer first, who would make a bold firm stand on the side of Holy Rus's messenger or against him. Few have the guts to truly be the first to go against the status quo.

As their mental gears churned, a heat signature appeared in his helm, and the noise of a badly maintained engine roared from the horizon. "A vehicle is approaching," he said to his fellow countrymen. The cowboys turned to look. Seeing black smoke, their heads whipped back. The plastic cowl fell from the head of the one in the center. His shaved bald head and weathered face could be that of a man of any age from twenty to fifty. With a grim look on his fleshless face, he quietly but firmly hissed at the Ultra Heavy, "Run down that hill and hide by the riverbank! Go, just go now, or you'll get all of us killed!"

Now it was #148 who was forced to make a quick yet final decision: have faith in this curious advice and wait this one out or confront whatever mechanized thing was coming for them. Time seemed to slow to a halt as he pondered… *No, it wasn't the time to shoot, but to listen*, he thought to himself. He quickly stumbled down the hill, careful to not let his knees bend the wrong direction. Shuffling downwards, he was able to see a decent spot where even he could hide easily.

Sitting on his rear end, he pushed himself with his hands under an alcove of rock next to a tiny creek. He unslung his machine gun and had it at the ready. The rock was thick and interfering with his helm's ability to see through materials, but he could hear everything on this silent, empty world. The occasional raindrop fell but this wouldn't stop his helm from eavesdropping via audio.

After some 45 seconds, the noise of the motor came very close and then someone turned off the engine. In the silence, the creaking open and slamming of a few doors was deafening in the infinite nothingness of Titan's surface. A few heavy steps of multiple entities moved, presumably closer to the plastic-wrapped horsemen.

"Boys, boys, boys, those cows there are lookin' mighty fine, oh that one there, with the black spots, what a dandy. I have to say you continue to outdo yourselves."

There was a moment of dead silence. Seeing nothing, our hero listened with volume increased nearly to maximum.

"Now, there's no reason to be so shy, guys. We've worked together for years now; you are truly reliable excellent employees. Zhores, hand out the bonuses..." A single set of footsteps was heard. "You see, your work here is always appreciated, but I have a question..."

There was more silence.

The main voice spoke with a superficially friendly but wicked tone, "Did you see anything fall from the sky?"

Seconds ticked away...

The answer from the cowboys broke the silence.

"No, Mr. President, no, we didn't see anything fall from the sky. Everything is the same as it always is: same cows, same grass, same sky."

"And how long have you been out here?"

"We've been out here for an eight-hour shift; it'll be over soon. We'll bring home the cows to rest. Tomorrow, we'll do some shoveling and get the converters right filled up!"

"You know, Stepan, I like you; you're an honest man, I can tell. So, how about this? Don't just sleep eight hours tonight. I'll pay you double-time for your next shift and let you take 24 hours off, but do me one small favor..."

Another pause, the type of silence that only a broken subordinate uses when addressing his master in fear...

"Um, what do you need us to do... sir?"

"Drive the cows home. Cover a lot of area. Go out there and look for anything unusual. It'll be an easy day at the office, deal?"

"No problem, boss, whatever you say!"

"Well, look at the time, you boys are off shift. If you want that bonus, get those cows home and start looking around for anything strange, would ya? Why, I do hope you'll vote for me in the next election, who else would pay you to go out on a stroll?" After this statement, he added in some obviously fake laughter.

The cowboys, in a broken unison, replied something

to the effect of "absolutely sir, you have our votes and our hearts!" With a gleaming tone, their boss replied, "Now that's the spirit; loyalty is a two-way street!"And with that, within the span of 30 minutes, every man, beast and machine had vanished, and our hero was alone under the alcove. The power of that voice was otherworldly. He could pierce the brain of any normal person with incredible ease. He was even beyond that of the porcelain god in his convincing verbal potency. Perhaps, he already knows that I'm here just from that conversation. #148 had to be careful, because something they called "the President" could potentially melt his brain before he even got the chance to shoot.

Looking up from under the rock alcove, he saw a small ship glowing as punched through the thin atmosphere. He was fairly certain that right now he was not the only one who would be watching the skies. Whoever was on the ship was far more likely to be an ally than an enemy. He stood, did a quick scan with his helm, confirming he was alone and began a brisk yet bumbling jog towards where the helm predicted the ship to land.

His weapon slung on his back, mace at his side in its magnetic sheath, he pumped his legs forward with small steps covering the broken terrain by the creek quickly.

Chapter 5: Help Arrives?

After moving some three kilometers as fast as he could, he was finally within normal eyesight of the spacecraft. It was one of ours, a small two-person craft, one-way capable only. It was the size of an escape pod and not a proper transport ship. He walked up to where one of the hatches should be located. The ship just went through the thick skies and was glowing hot on his thermal scans. He propped his machine gun into position just in case and waved his gauntlet over the external reader, trying not to get so close as to burn himself.

[Note from the Tsar: All Ultra-Heavies have extremely high-level clearance and any public building or imperial craft can be opened with their gauntlet, even if it were locked or seemingly encoded to restrict access to a limited few.]

As the hatch slowly lifted, it revealed a small frail woman kneeling, seemingly rummaging through personal belongings. She had long flowing blonde hair and was middle-aged. Her body looked petit and slender in her tight-fitting, dark-green uniform. Her hair was kept in place by a golden *kokoshnik* and similarly in gold was the symbol of the Ministry of Ideology over her heart.

"Oh, hi!" she said somewhat nervously at the gigantic dark figure pointing an automatic weapon at her—each round in his belt was nearly the length of the bone in her forearm. "Yeah, greetings," he replied coldly. The woman put her hands up in a sort of "don't shoot" pose and she spoke very carefully yet naively, "Are you… one of our guys?"

Lowering his gun, he answered with a monotone, "That is correct." The woman crawled forward on all fours to look out of the craft. Putting her hand on the frame of the hatch, she immediately pulled it back from the heat. Her face was striking, delicate with bright, wide eyes behind a layer of gentle wrinkles and weathering. She asked, "Um, why are you alone, where is everybody?" Our hero replied quickly and resolutely, "I can only assume that I was sent here alone, for the exact same reason that you were." "Oh!" she said, and seemed to quickly change the subject. "So, I was told there's all sorts of problems with the colony here and I… um… that is we… have to do something about it… um, like yeah." Now #148 peered into her tiny craft. There was some food and personal items, and two large cases marked as "clothing." "You came all the way out here, with no gun, and half your cargo is clothing… do you know something about this colony and this planet that I don't know?" She looked back a bit pouty with a furrowed brow and replied, "Hey, I do have a gun!" The lean woman in the twilight of her astounding beauty pulled a common 9x19 mm pistol from behind her back. It was the usual cold matte black in color. The weapon was seemingly unused as there was not a scratched edge to be seen. He let loose a long sigh, "A standard issue sidearm in the hands of a cheerleader from the Ministry of Ideology, let's hope the enemy likes to talk."

#148 could see from her reaction that perhaps he had gone too far with that last comment and formulated a more optimistic response to his own statement, "Look, I have reason to believe that some very violent individuals have been watching the sky. They know I landed but I doubt they found my craft. Your ship just lit up the sky like Moscow on December 31st. I've got two free hands. I'll take this case with food and one of these with your clothes." She looked grim and innocently asked, "But what am I going to do without half of my clothes?" Our hero leaned close to her face and through his helm uttered clearly, "You'll hang out at my ship half-naked... or would you rather stay here and get raped and murdered by the guys... or mutants... who are on their way here?" "Oh, um, then case #1 it is," she replied with a chirp. Grabbing the cases with ease, he pulled them out of the tiny craft. Then the lady departed through the hatch, careful not to burn herself. Just in case, #148 relocked the pod with his gauntlet and they began to move out.

They hiked for many kilometers.

"So, what's your name?" she asked. "Does it matter?" Our hero realized he was being too harsh to his only potential ally besides the cowboys, "They call me #148" She looked puzzled, staring up at him. "Your name is a number?" "The name I was born with was deleted from all records when I became an Ultra Heavy. I don't fully know why they do this, but those are the rules..."

[Note from the Tsar: I delete the names of the Ultra-Heavies primarily so no one could create a profile on whom I select and thus decode the selection process. If someone were to artificially create covert candidates for the Ultra Heavies, then just a few "planted individuals" could bring down our empire. A good AI could analyze the criteria and make any devil appear to be the perfect angel. There are some additional reasons mostly of a bureaucratic nature as well.]

"...but long story short, my birth name is gone; I am #148 now." "Um, do you have like a 'call sign' or something other than a number?" she asked, breathing deeply as she carried on beside him. Despite the need to "make friends," he was getting annoyed with the conversation. Over the centuries, he had had to have discussed this issue 10,000 times. The public was never fully made aware of the policies of the Ultra Heavies and so he had to clear this odd nuance up constantly, over and over. Then again, perhaps this instance would be the last time he had to explain his name being a number. That was certainly one of the perks from going on a suicide mission.

"Well, I do have a call sign. They call me 'Old-Timer' or at least they used to" "Oh! And why is that?" "Well, I have the lowest number left. I think #171 might be still around, but anyways, I'm probably the only one under #200… and thus I'm certainly next in line to die." Her large, bright eyes went wide looking up at him. "Don't say that!" He looked at her and after a pause replied, "Why not? It's true." "Well, just because it's true doesn't mean you have to say it!" He sighed, "Madam, I think Christ's suffering on the Cross proves otherwise. It is best we speak even ugly truths."

After this point, there was less talking.

[Redaction: A lot of time was spent to get to #148's craft, this has been omitted for brevity.]

Approaching his ship, he waved his gauntlet over the sensor to open it. "Computer, send a message converted to text from my speech to the Imperial Throne… Message start…"

[Redaction: He explained in great detail all the events that have occurred thus far.]

"Message end." He turned to the blonde girl and said, "Now you know everything, and they'll know everything. Let me go put a camo cloak over the ship. I can see it has already cooled off and no one will detect its heat, but this vessel definitely sticks out form the natural terrain." She glanced at him with bright eyes that were unopposed to the plan. "Sounds good, I guess!"

The ship was less than half full on power and the solar panels were yielding clownish results. #148 draped the ship with the cloak and set it to a standard setting This would use very little power, but would be nowhere as good as continuous adaptive camouflage, which chewed through batteries quickly. He started to play with the settings of the camo cloak. Both "Rock #12" and "Rock #13" were very convincing in appearance, but the former had just that right purplish tint that much of the dirt had here.

He returned to see what his female companion was doing inside. It took him quite some time to get the camo cloak just right by himself. He stepped into the ship, but he did so in just the wrong way. His knee twisted out of position by just a smidge over a millimeter. That one misstep was enough to send burning pain up his spine. Now was not the time to reveal his weakness to this "guest" and so he gritted his teeth and maintained his posture awkwardly frozen at the entrance.

He looked up to find that she had reorganized the cargo of the craft. Everything was tidy, and she had fashioned crates into a seating area and one as a kitchen. She had heated up tea… using valuable ship's energy in the process… but the smell was amazing. In the seating area on a large crate lay a plate with crackers perfectly arranged next to sliced cheese. #148 hadn't seen much action but he had been using his helm extensively and thus was quite hungry. Speaking of which, he removed his head protection and placed it on the ground, revealing his sand-blasted face to her for the first time.

"Oh, so that's what you look like! You don't even look that ancient, Old-Timer!" she said smiling. "Well, it's a cliché but it's true—'looks can be deceiving,' but anyways we talked about me a lot, so what's your name, girl?" She poured the tea into metal mugs in a slow gentle movement like a gymnast at the crescendo of a routine, "If you have a number and a call sign, well, I don't have a number but I do have a call sign too, mine is 'Klyookva' and that's what you can call me." For some reason she said these words with great pride. #148 tried to gather all of his politeness instincts and resist the urge to make a crude joke, "That is… a very adorable call sign, madam." "I think so too," she said smiling, looking at his scarred and battered face and trimmed long white beard.

"So… Klyookva… on Titan we are on nearly 16 Earth day cycles of day and night. I've been going for a while. Let me finish up this food and sleep for a few hours. When I wake up ,I think I know where the 'cowboys' I mentioned went. They seemed reluctant to cooperate. With the men in the vehicle, I think their camp or community or whatever may have allies. The problem is there could be spies there as well." Looking curious, she asked, "But how are you so sure?" He smiled a bit smugly, "My dear, I've cleared out a lot of Curse-ridden colonies in my day. There are 'tendencies' to how these things go down."

She seemed intrigued, "Oh, so what are some of those tendencies?" He smirked, "Well, I really want to get some sleep, but I can tell you this, for how much I'd love talk my way out of these crises, it usually means killing a lot of mutated freaks." He laid down on the floor like a dog and went to sleep. His companion pondered what "killing mutated freaks" would specifically entail and if she had the right stuff to do it.

She looked at this giant beast of a man at rest. *He's kind of a dick, but what a charming fellow, he knows everything!* she thought to herself.

Chapter 6: The Collective Ghost Town

Our duo of heroes made their way towards one of the second-tier heat signatures detected by #148's craft when it first landed. It was surely something related to human activity. The sky was still an orange-yellow swirl above a thin line of blue. The clouds were thick and bushy as usual. As they approached what seemed to be structures, the land smoothed out to becoming a perfectly flat plain covered in a thin, green coating of grass.

Near a few small trees was a network of standard shipping containers—angular, metal, and ubiquitous throughout Holy Rus'. Walking between them were a cow or two but more importantly there were people, living, breathing and seemingly non-'Cursed' in any external way. They were going about what looked to be an average day… for medieval peasants.

As they approached, the eyes of the children went wide. All of the locals were wearing somewhat ragged clothing and not a soul looked particularly well-fed. Cheek bones protruded and not a pot belly could be found among the lot. Then again, they certainly didn't appear to be dying of starvation either, which was a very positive sign.

An older woman, wearing a long dress, dirty at the bottom from brushing against the ground, rushed over. She wailed to the visitors, especially the more noticeable male visitor, "Our savior! The Tsar has sent us a savior!" #148 looked down at the woman hugging him around his waist. "Only Jesus Christ is the Savior. I am a combat-enhanced cyborg diplomat, but I do get the job done." The woman seemed quite confused by the response. His new female partner gently removed the frantic woman from his waist and wagged her finger towards her, making a "no-no" type of motion.

A man exiting one of the containers cried out, "Foolish woman, the Tsar is a lie; he died centuries ago! That metal skeleton sitting on the Throne is a rogue AI! The empire has been enslaved by thinking machines! And it was that Tsar-robot who fucked us all, who fucked each and every one of us here on Titan! He sent us to this shithole planet with no plan, no support and no nothing! You, hag, are blinded by gilded helmets and fancy uniforms! What can he do for us? Look at these two clowns dressed up for a masquerade," he said as he violently pointed at them. "Why'd you come here alone? Did the AI on the Throne make another accounting error?" And with those words, the objectionable man began to laugh like the worst actor at the local theater.

"That is a fair question." #148 looked at this man directly, breathing in slowly. He was an older gent with a mustache of gray, a linen *rubakha* and wide pants clearly three sizes too big, tied to his waist with a belt made of some strange material. "Yes, I assure you that I have come under the direct order of the Tsar and that his brain is very much made of flesh and not the coding of artificial intelligence. But I can do nothing for your community if I have no idea what has gone wrong here. Let's all work together here. So for starters, why are you living in shipping containers?"

This small mustache-man began to blurt his answer as a crowd of every local began to gather to witness the rare commotion. "It's because you… you and your wise pseudo-Tsar gave up on us. You never sent the second ship. The third ship should have arrived last year, and where is it? Where is our technology? Where are all the robots to do this work for us? Where are our prefab homes? Your metal skeleton freak just wanted a public relations triumph to sweep the news. That's what his algorithm told him! He just wanted to make it look like something in Unholy Rus' was happening when NOTHING EVER HAPPENS in the empire! You do NOTHING; you produce NOTHING; you represent a fake nation of eternal repression. You're the guards at the prison of peoples!" With that, half of the crowd started to cheer in praise while others remained notably silent. The angry local was spitting as he spoke like a rabid dog finally being able to throw his anger and frustration at something.

#148 felt a finger poking him in the waist. Looking down, Klyookva was making faces, hinting for him to let her whisper something in his ear via frantic hand gestures. He bent over and through his helm heard: "His mind has been tainted; he is being manipulated." "How do you know that?" "I've scanned a lot of possessed people's minds over the years. There are tendencies."

#148 knew that the Ministry of Ideology did use 3D chemistry in attempts to expand the mind, but this came as a bit of a surprise. The man in gigantic trousers continued his tirade, pleading to the audience and becoming more and more oblivious to his actual opponents in the dialogue. Any attempts to discuss anything of value were immediately shifted to the topic of the Tsar being bad, fake or repressive. He had nothing substantive to say but his conviction to these false pretexts seemed as deep as a canyon. Everything simply swung back to more insults—*vatnik*, *moscal'*, slaves of the skeleton and so on.

Our man asked his female companion quietly, "Is there anything you can do about this mental possession? I don't think reason or violence will work here." She bit her lip and responded, "Well, the problem is that if I try, it'll look like I'm murdering him." #148 clenched his fist. "Then that's a no go… for now."

With arms spread, the mustachioed orator continued, "If it wasn't for President Fleischman, we'd have nothing. He brought us freedom from your eternal backwards tyranny. He gave us what we have! He banished the superstitions of old! He freed us from the tyranny of Moscow! he gave us liberty!" He then pointed his finger at our hero almost like a pistol, and staring down the barrel, he spoke, "And you sir, the longer your empire stays away, the more prosperity we'll have here… be gone with you!"

These words were met with roaring applause… by some.

"It is you and your Tsars that have kept us down, kept us from evolving into greater beings, kept us from just enjoying life, with your foolish duties. Everything that is wrong with this planet is because of your leader and his *vatnik* Russian slaves. We'd be living as good as the Fascists if not for you!"

Hooting, howling, and applause continued after every finished statement as if on cue.

#148 took a deep breath and stepped forward. He began to bark at the audience in the loud terrifying voice of the cybernetic goliath that he was. "The fact that you never received a second ship nor the things you were promised disgusts me as much as it disgusts you. You have been wronged. But that is no reason to break away from Holy Rus'. I am in direct contact with the Tsar. We can put together a plan of action. Within a very short time, I am sure we can at least begin to construct a proper colony with a high… post-medieval minimum standard of living. This I assure you, I give you my word before God that this is the case!"

The man with the mustache and flopping trousers bent over, slapped his thigh and hooted, "Well, guess what? Fuck your God! And fuck you, pal!" And then he began laughing manically.

#148 could hear heckling. One man yelled, "Fuck you, you meat slave of the metal tyrant!" A teenager joined in, "Go back to Moscow, *vatnik*!" Another added, "His promises will never happen. He's a liar sent to take what we have!"

"What can I do, right now, to prove to you, that I mean what I say? Is there not a problem that I can solve for you, as a gesture of good faith?"

"Kill the damn goo monsters!" yelled the woman who had hugged him.Suddenly the tone of the rabid crowd changed...

"They've killed three cows. If they kill any more, we're all dead!" Some of the hecklers seemed intrigued by the offer. "Yeah, go ahead, see how well you do against them. Good luck pal!" Another one yelled, "If you can beat them, we'll make YOU the Tsar!" Klyookva, staring into their eyes, could see that there was truth behind their programmed sarcasm: these goo monsters really were an existential threat. When push comes to shove, it takes a hell of a lot of elite-level propaganda to defeat an existential threat in someone's mind. As an employee of the Ministry of Ideology, she knew this all too well.

The little woman peering from under her gold *kokoshnik* looked deeper into the mind of the man with the mustache specifically. She could see that the mental programming didn't take into account this "olive branch" maneuver by #148. His conscious mind wanted to fight the offer, but there were no talking points to rebut it. Furthermore, he truly believed that if a major number of cows were to die, humanity on this planet would go extinct. This was again the power of truth that no propaganda could outweigh. #148 was either a brilliant orator, was being led by divine providence or he just got very lucky. No food means no life and none of these locals were willing to die to spite the Tsar... yet. Food trumps supposed "freedom."She again poked #148, "It's working; you've broken through the lies."Now it was our hero's turn to engage in theatrics. Knowing only to himself that he was being ridiculous, he struck an aggressive pose and began to bellow forth his declaration, "You, respected citizen, show me where this mutant infestation is and I shall rid the land of it. Your livestock will be safe, all of it. You shall live, and based on this, we shall begin to mend the wounds between the empire and your colony."

The crowd reacted with quiet skepticism.

Returning to his more natural demeanor, he turned to the woman in the long dirty dress that had embraced him and said, "Alright, let's go." Our heroes turned their backs to the bitter mob and began to walk away.

The man with the mustache wanted to continue the argument but lacked the words. He started to mumble, "Well, okay, if you get rid of the mutants, then, we can talk, but you'll never do it! It's impossible; they're too strong. You should have stayed on Earth, slave boy!"

[Redaction: A lot of walking was done.]

Our heroes and the woman still loyal to Moscow kept going on the long march to the source of the so-called "goo monsters." The older woman began to rant as they walked. "Oh, it's horrible, it's horrible! These liquid monsters have taken over the best meadow on the whole planet, the one place where grass grows well. Ugh, that's where they always are! The cows just think they are mud or something. The poor dears don't know the danger! Our shepherds are at a loss as of what to do. The darn bovines are driven by a mad hunger. The grass here cannot be resisted; it is a delicacy for them!" Although she was making sense, the overall word soup was turning into a monotone wailing that needed to stop in the opinion of our core hero.

"So..." #148 said loudly and abruptly, "Could you tell me who 'President Fleischman' is? That term hasn't been used by our side for about 2,000 years now, so who is this 'president' and what does he 'preside' over exactly?" She looked slightly nervous, not quite looking him in the visor. They continued to walk and she started to explain chaotically, "Well, I wasn't born here. Then again, few have been. I arrived with most of the others already as an adult, so I remember it clearly... I think. So when we arrived, Prince Zhukov got really sick. His body just couldn't handle the new air... you know the air now is actually better than it used to be... my sister always tells me 'oh, the air is still bad' but then I tell her..."

"Could you be more specific about how Prince Zhukov died?" #148 grunted. She shook her head and continued, "Well, he just got sicker and sicker and then he... died. Some other people got sick from the air too, but only Zhukov died. I guess he was too old or something. So then, after that, we had a vote, and we made Fleischman the acting prince. He ran the ship that got us here, so people looked up to him. Also he has a way with words. It reminds me of my uncle who used to play *durak* during the winters in..."

"So Fleischman was captain of the ship but not the colony?" She continued her murmuring, "He has become very popular, but I have my doubts. He told us that if we didn't reorganize quickly, we'd all die. He said that 'being determines consciousness' and that we couldn't live by the Tsar's rules on this wild planet. You know, everything has to adapt to survive, like Darwin said. Later, he told everyone the Tsar is dead, or that he is an AI, or both, and they believed him! I remember the Tsar told many funny anecdotes. No AI could do that. Now, my cousin, he used to work with AI down at the university on Ganymede and boy oh boy did he tell me about how..."

[Redaction-]

"...but you know what, Fleischman's 'democracy' isn't that great, but gosh darn it, none of the other ships came. What were we supposed to do?... Fleischman did sort of save us from dying."

[Note from the Tsar: It is true that the ships were not sent. Unfortunately, some typical "external and internal strife" began nearly at the time the Titan colony's second vessel was to be launched. In the future, it would be wise to allocate funds and resources for such ventures in advance. This is another great error during my reign that should not be repeated.]

#148 calmed the old woman down with a soothing tone, "So, Fleishman told you that Moscow's rules didn't apply here because no more colony ships came, right? But then why are you living in shipping containers? What's the logic?"

Regardless of his words, she continued on with a tornado of syllables and emotions, "And so, he told us about how in the olden days they had collective farms where all the workers got the benefits from the farm equally. The farms belonged to the farmers! This was just like this book we read when I was in school in Izhevsk…

[Redaction-]

…so we were all excited about liberty and getting the 'means of production' in our hands, especially my sister who gets very excited about things. We would become the rugged individuals this planet needs! This sounded great and we all agreed, but to be honest, I don't really get it anymore. We seem to do a lot, but don't get much in return. The Board of Distribution says it will give us everything we need if we just follow the plan, but it doesn't ever seem to. My sister keeps telling me that we need to stick to the plan. We have so much more freedom now than under Moscow. No one has to serve in the army, and there's no morality *druzhinas*, but I don't know… all I do is gather cow poop all day. so I feel that we should…"

His female companion entered into the conversation and they began to continue the storm of words together. #148 hoped that she could perhaps provide some sort of summary translated from 'womanese' at a later point. The one thing he could say for sure was this Fleischman fellow was blasting the locals with every flavor of egotistical ideology that he could to turn them against the imperial status quo. This was probably to make himself the lord of this realm. Men are biologically driven to raise their status as high as it can go, often at the expense of others.
The Old-Timer could see something from within his helm. It looked like one of the 'cowboys' was on the horizon. "Hold that thought, ladies," he said to the gabbing women. The rider seemed to be waiting about 300 meters out from the valley they were quickly approaching. *Let him watch. He doesn't even have a gun. It won't make a difference,* he thought to himself. He also noticed while heat-scanning that one of his female companion's legs was vastly colder than the rest of her body, a rather unusual anomaly, but there was no time to ponder or inquire about its nature right this moment.

The three of them approached what looked more like a large crater than a "valley." It was a vast circular shape, probably a kilometer or more in diameter with a drop off at the edges of about the height of a man. However, there were a few spots where the edge was much lower, maybe to knee height. That is surely where the cows could easily get in one by one and he could see why they'd want to. The bottom of the crater was absolutely lush with grass. It was thick and green like in the lower regions of the Altai Mountains back home. It was impressive that by God's will we could create such dense vegetation 9.5 AU away from the Sun! He performed the sign of the cross slowly, showing gratitude to his Creator and this scientific miracle. But then he noticed something odd.

In the exact center of the crater was a pool of dark liquid. If it were water being only ankle-deep, you'd be able to see the bottom, but it was pitch black with glossy edges and completely opaque. He turned to the woman collective farmer… "Is that the 'goo monster' you spoke of?" She looked at him with honesty and confusion, "Well, it was my cousin's son who saw it firsthand, but I mean maybe, he said they were 'black and shiny' and well, that looks black and shiny! Although it doesn't' look like a monster." The woman put her hand to her face to try to remember all the stories she was told about the creatures that dwell here.

#148 turned and looked at her directly, "Mutations can take all manner of form, but there are tendencies." He hopped down the sharp edge of the crater landing on the soft grass and delicate soil. He drew his machine gun from his back and put it into firing position. He yelled to the women, "Stay up there and stay silent."

He approached the black glimmering pool. Our hero took in a deep breath and spoke in his most official and intimidating voice, adding some artificial rasp, "Respected entity, I represent the will of the Tsar of Holy Rus'. On his behalf I wish to negotiate a…" As he spoke, the pool started to change shape quickly, forming a cauldron of blackness around him. He quietly started to pace backwards.

Suddenly a human-like form emerged from the black oily slop. Our hero quickly side-stepped it only for another to appear all too close. He turned his torso with great force, thrashing at it with the butt on his machine gun. Another arose and being off balance he kicked it with a stomp, knocking it down and back into the central pool.

Another one tried to grab the arm holding his gun as it popped out from seemingly nowhere. *How can man-sized creatures fit in 10cm of used motor oil?* he thought to himself as he started to shake off the monsters trying to grab him. He could feel as they embraced him that somehow a human skeleton was inside of all that black goo. There was something crunchy within them.

After playing contact football for many years, he knew the feeling when a defensive player's arm got locked under his armpit being bent the wrong way. In that moment, it meant his opponent had the choice to either give up and be out of the play, or get his arm snapped in two. The tar-coated beings were surrounding him more and more, and so he put all his strength into pinning the gooey arm that was now trying to steal his gun. He was forcing it towards the breaking point, and yet more and more of these tar-covered men continued to rise from seemingly nowhere. Then, with a twist of his torso, he ripped the arm completely off, freeing up his machine gun.

A cacophony of screams was wailed by the entity. "Why did you do that? It hurts! Stop it!" the concert of various voices yelled. The ooze started to retreat back to its original position. #148 held the jet-black lifeless arm in his left hand. He pointed it at the pool of goo like a school teacher at the chalk board. "Back off right now! Why do you keep killing cows? What's the point of all this? Is there nothing else to eat? Why attack me? What did I ever do? Are you that hungry?"

The collective pool replied with voices coming from various humanoid shapes within it: "Give us back that arm! I want my arm! That's not yours!" Heads, shoulders and torsos of a liquid nature all rose out of the central pool starting at #148 as they spoke. Our hero replied, "I'll give it back, when we work out a deal Why do you kill the cows that come through here? What the hell do you want!?"

The response was a somewhat joyful "We do it, cause they're delicious, cows are tasty, beef… it's what's for dinner!" #148 held the arm up in the air away from the pool like someone playing "keep away" with their dog as some of the creatures started to come closer. "So why kill me then? Am I also tasty?" The pool of goo monsters shook its heads unanimously from side to side. "Well, you have a gun, we don't, nope we have no gun, that gun is very cool."

"Well, gentlemen, it is very cool, but could you promise to perhaps try to go somewhere and eat something else?" The pool responded with many statements but the loudest voice said, "Yes, but nothing else comes through the crater, only cows, and they are tasty." #148 took a careful breath, "So you have to be in this crater for some reason? Why?"

The twenty or so lurching humanoid goo monsters shook their heads from side-to-side, "No, no, you don't get it, you don't understand... we don't want to be here, I hate this place, this place sucks, but the cliff is steep, it's too damn high."#148 was baffled by his own reasoning. He replied speaking slowly and dragging his words, "So... you mean to say that because you are partially liquid it is hard for you to go uphill, you fell into this crater and can't get out? Are you stuck here, is that it?" All of the creatures nodded in agreement.

"So how about this... if I dig you a way out of this ditch, you'll leave and go eat the other animals on this planet and NOT cows of any kind. Do we have a deal?" The pool pondered for a moment, "Um, okay, yes, we promise, can I have my arm back? Our buddy misses his arm so much." The Ultra Heavy tossed the arm to the member of the collective entity that he ripped it from. The creature let out a childlike "hooray!" and reattached it.

"Okay, boys, we've got a deal. I'll dig you out of here. It'll take me a while to do this because I've got to go get a shovel, but then you'll leave and only eat non-people and non-cows, right?" The pool quickly agreed, "Deal, I agree, sounds good, okay."

#148 wanted to try his luck, "One more thing: do any of you gents happen to know anything about a man named Fleischman?" The pool spoke with utter disinterest to the non-pertinent question, "That name sounds familiar, yeah I heard it once, me too, boring question, who cares?"

Klyookva, overhearing all of this, pranced up to the

edge of the crater. "You did it, and you didn't even have to kill anyone." He responded with a sigh, "Yeah, but now I am going to have to walk all the way back and get a shovel and dig for hours. Maybe I should have just shot them?"

From his flank, #148 sensed a metal object flying towards him. He heard words from a male human voice: "Will this do?" #148 caught the object turning his torso around—it was a portable trench shovel. It was the "cowboy" voyeur who threw it to him. He spoke from under his plastic cowl in the dim daylight, "Look man, I appreciate what you're trying to do here, but you don't know what you're up against. The President is not going to be so easily convinced as these delightful folks in the crater. He, with his men, took control of all the resources of the first colony ship as soon as Zhukov died. He has all the guns and all the converters. We work, so he can convert our cow shit into everything HE needs, and he gives us just enough to get by. Love him or hate him, we're stuck with him, because he holds all the cards."

Klyookva seemed annoyed by this reasoning, "Well, where's your imperial spirit? Why don't you rise up against him or steal the converters in the night?" With obvious sarcasm in his voice, he answered, "Didn't you just hear, girl? He has all the guns!" Our hero chimed in to his lady friend, "And people never rise up; they are risen up by outside forces." The cowboy continued, "Yeah, something like that, and you look to be quite the 'outside force' but there is nothing to rise up for. You guys threw us on the trash heap of history. What would getting rid of Fleischman do? It wouldn't change the fact that we have 3 converters for an entire planet and he who controls them, and the guns, controls us. There is no way to leave; nothing will change; we're trapped here forever at his mercy."

#148 took a sigh to contain his inner rage at the "pity party" being thrown by the mounted shepherd. "Look, I was sent here to solve the problem with this colony by any means necessary. You can sit on the sidelines and not risk your neck if you want, but I need details. Where is Fleischman? Where are his converters? How many fighting men does he have?" The man on horseback rattled off the answers dispassionately. "He operates out of 'London.' That's the area around the ship that brought us here. It's north of the collective farm you visited. All the important resources, like the converters, are still inside the ship. We produce enough manure for him to convert and keep the lights of the ship on. He probably has thirty or so guys working directly for him, doing 'collections' and making sure no one gets out of line."

"Oh, that's good info! But why are you telling this to us?" Klyookva asked. "Because I hate that fucker Fleischman, and well, maybe we'd all be better off dead than in his service. Your boyfriend here should be able to get the job done." The lady from a far-off land stomped and pouted, "He's not my boyfriend!"#148 took a deep breath at the compliment of sorts. "I appreciate the kind words, but fighting thirty guys at once won't go well, even for me." The man under the plastic tarp shrugged, "I just want to see the President's dead body, whatever info you need from me to get that job done, I'll give it to you… good luck, homie." The rider turned around and rode off into the distance.

"Well, ladies, I've got some shoveling to do!" The collective farm woman asked a storm of questions in the newfound silence, "So you're going to kill Fleischman? How are you going to dig all of this? Won't your back hurt? I promise not to tell anyone, not even my sister! Maybe I should help you?"

#148 raised his hand, "Look, lady, just go home and don't tell anyone what was discussed here today. Just tell them the goo guys will be gone soon. I want some peace and quiet, alright?"

Klyookva put her bare hand against the skull of the

woman. She stared intently into her eyes. #148 merely overlooked the spectacle. The local woman collapsed sitting on the ground in a daze. Klyookva, smiling, said, "Now she won't remember anything!" "Impressive," he replied.

[Redaction: The hours of shoveling needed to free the entity from the fertile crater is not necessary information.]

Chapter 7: An Audience with the President

As they made their way back to the collective farm, it didn't take the omniscient vision of #148's helm to see that something was out of the ordinary. Again, the town of bored farm laborers was all gathered together, but this time around the epicenter of their gathering was a large truck with an orange cabin parked in the center of the makeshift town.

The vehicle sat quite high off the ground, with two wheels in front and two sets of two in the back. The boxy compartment for goods in the rear was gray and clearly came from some other factory or as an add-on, looking completely different from the bright tangerine cab. Everyone turned their heads in unison as our heroes made their "triumphant" return to the settlement.

"The goo is gone," #148 said to the crowd. A few of them made the sign of the cross in stunned reaction. Hearing these words, some men wearing dingy blue uniforms from the civilian transport fleet moved out from around the truck. The imperial eagle that should be over their heart was replaced by some sort of dark blue looping design over a yellow rectangle. Not surprisingly, the tricolor was absent from their shoulder as well.

"Who are they?" his young female companion asked quietly, peering out from behind his massive frame. Keeping his voice down, he replied, "Fleischman was captain of the colony ship. Perhaps he convinced the crew to sign up for his 'revolutionary mission' or those were simply the only uniforms they had access to and he just gave them to whomever was loyal."

The collective farm woman, still dazed from having her memory wiped, quietly disappeared back into the mass of bodies, while all the burning attention was being thrown at the outsiders. She could feel in her bones that now was not the best time to stand out from the crowd.

One of them seemed to be in charge, walking in front of the others with a smug smile and cocky strut. His blue and white sailor's hat was gently tipped back in a slovenly way on his head. He, like the others, held an assault rifle in his hands. It was one of the seemingly endless versions of the AK platform that We've been using for millennia. Who knows how many worlds and adventures that weapon had seen?

The unique smile on the "sailor's" face was something our hero knew well—it was the sign of a weak man finally getting the chance to feel strong. Every envious runt takes far too much pleasure in playing the role of the alpha. "Well, where have you been? We've been waiting for YOU!" he said with fake kindness. #148 replied, "I had to unclog a toilet." That answer baffled the man in the uniform, but he returned to smug confident form quickly. As they spoke, the horde of locals hung on every word, watching as if it were a sporting event.

Klyookva tried to peruse the minds of these minions. She poked at her companion and quietly quipped, "They're all true believers, 100% under his spell." "Lovely," the Ultra Heavy said quietly with deep cold sarcasm.

"Hey, don't you ignore me, boy! President Fleischman requests your presence. You get in the back of the truck now... but your lady friend can ride up front with me." The other men in is squad cackled, hooted and hollered at the thought. "She rides with me in the back," #148 said in a steely cold tone. The squad leader took off his hat and performed an elegant bow as if he had just ended an opera while saying, "As you wish… you are the honored guest after all!" #148 really wanted to wipe the grin off of his face, but now was not the time. Now was the time to figure out if Fleischman was the problem or just a small part of the problem.

Guiding his lady friend by the shoulder, they moved around to the back of the truck, parting the crowd as they walked. He lifted her onto the back, grabbing her waist and gently launching her like a ballerina leaping with her partner's assistance.

The bald man with gigantic pants came out of the woodwork and spoke like a carnival barker, "You see I knew these *vatniks* were bad news, and President Fleischman knows it too. He'll set these losers straight for sure!" Hearing these words, the more "patriotic" members of the shipping-container-based collective farm began to hop up and down as if they had achieved something. They saw this as a victory, but at the same time, the most terrifying and powerful man on the planet was about to make contact with their frail leader. Only the very short-sighted on their side could have rejoiced at this moment and yet most seemed to be ecstatic.

#148 pushed himself up onto the back of the truck to join his lady friend. Two of the squad went into the cabin of the truck while three sat in back. The engine came to life and the vehicle began to drive away. Now that they were at a safe distance, the villagers flashed their middle fingers at the messenger of the Tsar and his companion. They jeered and hollered. The lady in the long dirty dress who went with them to the crater slowly waved goodbye in a ghostly manner. She did the sign of the cross to wish them blessings on their dangerous journey. No one from the crowd bore witness to this, although many of them should have been fated to have seen it.

Now that the odds were lowered, Klyookva could feel the arrogance of the men transform into a passive fear.

These space sailors were now waking up to the fact that they were stuck in a small cage with a large gorilla. She sensed that more and more they wanted to jump out as they stared at the hulking cybernetic beast glaring them down in pure silence. The unblinking gaze of his helm was eating away at their arrogance.

But she was not a fan of silence, especially when she was scared. She looked at the Ultra Heavy and began to speak quietly, "You know, I…" He immediately cut her off, "Yes, I know that you want to have time to wash your underwear. Stop reminding me; we'll get to it." At first, she didn't get it… she paused to think… but quickly took the hint, "Oh, yeah, sorry for being a bother. I'm just running out." The two "prison guards" looked out of the sides of their eyes at this strange conversation but said nothing.

As the vehicle hopped up and down going over bumps and rocks, one bolt was bouncing around on the floor. It looked to be a 10x70 mm bolt made of a more traditional form of steel. #148 casually caught it on the bounce like a fumbled contact football. He squeezed it with his hand, bending the bolt into mush as if it were made of clay. The two ship crewmen's eyes lit up at the spectacle. "Are you sure you don't want to rethink your imperial citizenship, boys?" our hero asked quietly. They said nothing but sat as far away as they could from him, guns at the ready.

[Redaction: Nothing of interest happened until they arrived at the ship.]

The truck drove up the drop ramp of the huge ship and into the outer hull. All of a sudden, the ride got quite smooth. Entering the vessel, everything also became even dimmer than usual. From the back of the truck, our heroes could see the grand scale of the vessel looming over them and the big potential that it brought to Titan. They were like fish looking out from inside the mouth of an iron whale.

Curiously, they could clearly see that some kind of work was going on near the ship, but interestingly enough everyone who was dressed like the locals was working a lot, and everyone in a "sailor suit" was merely watching them—many with gun in hand. It was unclear what they were doing but apparently heavy things in boxes needed to be moved to and fro and only a certain class of people were destined to move them.

The guards sort of slid their way out first, keeping their bodies pointed towards the "guests," just in case. All of these civilian transport space vehicles were essentially the same but were far more impressive in person than their dull design looked on a monitor. They were built to withstand a hell of a lot of damage while they made their journey. Titan's atmosphere was even more vicious to spacecraft than Earth's and this thing must have taken an absolute pounding from the heat during entry into the atmosphere.

Each transport ship of this class, regardless if it was used for colonization or not, was structured in the following way from stern to bow in a straight line:

- The outer hull with drop ramp for loading and unloading of basic cargo
- The engine room (engineering)
- Fuel reserves/tanks
- The inner hull: for higher priority, delicate or critical cargoCrew quarters
- The bridge: where all command functions and computer systems lie

Each hull was usually the size of a contact football field with the other sections being much smaller, especially the bridge. It was very dark on the inside, like a metallic crypt with artificial lighting. Windows were kept to a minimum and restricted to the bridge and crew quarters, where they would be of use. Unlike most humans, shipping containers do not suffer mentally from space travel and thus are crammed in tightly into pure cold darkness.

As #148 left the back of the truck, he took a moment to look around via his helm: everything was very standard issue, but there was some weird nonsense additional wiring all over the place. But shockingly for a ship designed to start a new community on a new planet, it seemed like nothing had changed here since it landed.

[Note from the Tsar: There is much confusion among the public as to what a colony ship actually is. Although we could build ships that would be able to travel both to and from another colony, this is highly inefficient. No matter how much the Academy of Sciences tries to pressure You, do not invest into this foolish project or two-way colony ships. An empty colony ship above all functions as a power plant. Organic matter gets dumped into converters; they convert it to fuel; that fuel is loaded into the tanks of the ship, and thus the ship can generate power to an entire community. Thus, one-way ships provide stable and powerful energy projection, so long as there is organic matter to be found. Thus, the epicenter of every new colony is always its first ship.

Furthermore, once the goods for the community are unloaded from the ship, the hulls, quarters and bridge can be used for all sorts of public functions. The inner hulls of all ships made within the last few generations can easily be converted into a church with the raising of an iconostasis into marked locations. The bridge of the first colony ship on Ganymede was used as the local prince's Throne for quite some time. That ship's outer hull hasbeen used as a market of sorts to this day.]

The guards, some of them more cautious than before, led them to the doors that went deeper into the linear vessel. The card-access system on the pad next to the thick pressure-resistant metal doors seemed to have been completely unaltered. *Why would they have just left this as is? #148* thought to himself, *I can open every door in the ship at a whim. Could they be that stupid or did they never expect any guests from Moscow?* As the crewman swiped their cards, he could see that, indeed, the OS remained untouched. The doors slowly but smoothly opened for them.

From the titanic outer hull, filled with a priceless fortune of public goods, never distributed to the public, they continued on to engineering. Normally, the engine room is a fascinating yet miserable place. It is a chamber of constant heat and abysmal, unending noise. It is a place that an Ultra Heavy or member of the Ministry of Ideology would consider themselves blessed not to work in. It took a certain type of character to work as an engineer and, judging by the quiet in the room, perhaps no one on this planet currently had such a mind. #148 continued his inner monologue, *They must be using a sub engine to power the lights and computer, but are they saving fuel, or are the actual engines busted, or were the noise and smells just too much to bear?*

He looked down at his co-adventurer and it didn't take elite cybernetic implants to tell that she was extremely nervous. He had been in the belly of the beast many times. She was clearly "unhappy," marching blindly into the devil's lair, with steel doors shutting behind them with a thud, locking them into what could be their doom. He placed his gloved hand on her shoulder to help her calm down. *Everything will be fine. I've got this,* he thought clearly in his mind, hoping she would hear the words. Judging by her reaction—she did.

Through his helm, he could again see that strange additional wiring was here too. It was all linked down a single pathway along the spine of the ship. The wiring was cheap like it came from home appliances. But what was most interesting was that it was connected at roughly

10-meter intervals… to explosives. Not just fireworks, but "the good stuff," with all sorts of nails and screws in plastic bags taped over it but quite well hidden from normal vision.

He took his arm off of his lady friend for mental privacy. *Is this some form of defense? Why bother with these toys of terrorism, when it is just as likely to kill your own guys? With one good electric pulse, going down the entire length of the ship, this whole damn spacecraft would turn into an inferno of explosions, killing everyone, and probably setting off the fuel tanks from within. This is utterly stupid… or maybe did someone sneak in here and set this up undetected? Perhaps there are more angry locals than just that one old chatty woman? How has the crew never found all these devices? Do they never do maintenance? Or, are some of them in on it?* This encounter with Fleischman was dangerous enough, but now it was hard to shake from his mind the fact that he was walking through a literal minefield.

Moving through the fuel reserves, he could see they were at 25% capacity, which, given they only kept the lights on, was actually a very substantial amount. If someone wanted to send messages to Moscow, a lack of energy to do so was not the issue at all. Then again, he hadn't seen the condition of the communications station. Perhaps it was busted?

From there, they approached another security door labeled "inner hull." The leader of the squad of crewmen opened it with his card but this time, as the doors moved, he, with great theatrics, bowed, showing the way in to his "honored guests from Moscow." While the crewman wasted time with mind games, #148 noticed on the panel that it said he was "number 8 of 37," meaning that in theory only about forty people actually served on the ship. Then again, perhaps that data comes from the start of their journey; maybe now there were far more… or hopefully from our heroes' perspective… far less. Then #148 remembered something as he thought to himself, *The cowboy was right; he was telling the truth. There are a little over thirty of them, too many for a direct assault... on my own... but with a distraction... with some support... their asses are fucked... if it comes to that, that is.* Sensing this explosion of optimism... and bloodlust... Klyookva turned and gave him a puzzled look. He gently shook his head to signal to her "it's nothing."They stepped into a vast room with gorgeous cathedral ceilings culminating in arches and a central dome far above their heads. Interestingly, they were painted white in a very sloppy manner, seemingly with the wrong kind of paint as flakes had fallen off, leaving specs of original bright colors. It was a sloppy attempt to whitewash what used to be there.

To the extent that his helm could penetrate the metal containers around him, he could see they had large storages of food, somehow still from their initial journey. There were many tools, clothing, and technological supplies unopened in the original packaging. And most importantly of all, there were plenty of weapons, but it was clear that those containers had not remained sealed. Considering the Curse hadn't caused any... "major" problems here in that regard... these arms had probably only been used against their countrymen.

From there, they walked through the open doors to the crew quarters which, unlike the rest of the ship, were bathed in warm pleasant lighting that shone through the thick metal doorway.

The repugnant leader of the guard squad looked up at #148, "You should be respectful to Fleischman. You may think you're hot shit now, but if Mr. President gives the order... and I hope he does... we'll blow your slave-driving ass to bits! In other words, mind your manners, Muscovite cunt!" "I am always polite," #148 answered coldly, not giving a millimeter to the attempted trolling. "We'll see," the leader of the guard said mockingly as he pointed the way with both hands and glaring with a villainous smile.

As they passed into the most human chamber of the big metal beast, a grand hall was revealed. This was the living space for all the many hundreds of colonists to sleep, relax and survive before and after landing on a new world. Sleeping through the journey saves time and reduces the risks of space travel, but someone had to be awake and make sure everything was in working order. Thus, in the distance it was visible how this area was divided into many rooms along the sides for those who were awake and pods in the middle for the more impatient and weak-stomached of the passengers who slept. They were of the exact same type that #148 had arrived in. Our hero got the feeling that these chambers were now the only luxury real estate on Titan controlled by the planet's new "revolutionary" elite.

As our heroes entered, one of the women from the collective farm mopped the floor around them. "Move your feet, would ya?" she said in a shrill demanding voice as she tried to wipe away any dirt they may have tracked in. Another in the distance was cleaning up dishes and cups on a far off table. But it was hard to notice these minor details as their attention was easily drawn to the center of this compartment of the ship.

Sitting upon a welded metal throne sat a thin man in a fine navy blue suit with yellow tie. His hair was just as dark as his blazer, and it was shoulder length, slicked back by some oil. Given they were on a freshly colonized world, it must have been actual motor oil. His frame and face were thin and surprisingly and very unusual for a male citizen of Holy Rus'... he was completely clean-shaven.

He gave off the vibe of some businessman who may have lost the plot years ago, sitting like the mad hatter on a makeshift throne. But, more importantly, surrounding him were two separate squads of spacefaring sailors—some with assault rifles. But sadly, on the upper level, he could see the bane of his existence as an Ultra Heavy: anti-tank rockets in the arms of men who despised him, not even knowing who he was or his intentions.

[Note from the Tsar: Perhaps, my Heir, You should consider not providing heavy weapons to colonists. The likelihood of them encountering some giant beast, tank piloted by Southerners, or Fascist bio construct is quite small. And to my great sorrow, when our citizens feel betrayed, as can be the case under the constant threat of death as a fresh colony emerges… they can misplace their frustrations onto our organs of state power. We should stick with civilian rifles. They are a great reliable choice.]

#148 knew that the segments of his over-armor could stop one incoming rocket at a time, but not four, and even the finest *troika* steel, with this "wiggling flexibility on impact," couldn't deflect that much force entirely. If there was to be a fight today, it had best remain a war of words as our hero was at too strong of a disadvantage—he hadn't forgotten what transpired at the Martian car factory. #148 noticed that one of them went to fetch what looked like a particle-beam cannon. This was definitely becoming really bad odds.

"Well, well, look at this, friends, we have an imperial slave driver *vatnik* extraordinaire, one of the great ass-lickers of the metallic, skeletal AI megalomaniac! What a pleasure it is to meet a man of your status! It's not every day you meet someone who's sucked the dick of the most powerful unloving man in the System!" Fleischman snapped his fingers upon finishing his words and sat up from his relaxed position.

When confronted with trolling and provocation, "defusing" the situation with stoic, cold speech is a reliable oratory tactic and one that #148 implemented well. "Speaking of the Tsar, he sent me to find out what happened here, so could you be so kind as to tell me what happened to the Titan colony?" Fleischman put his hand to his chest, pretending to act aghast at the question like a lady of the elite at a Venetian ball. "Where is your deep Russian soul? What is this 'down to business' attitude? I thought a bit of casual conversation always preceded serious dealings? Russian foreplay is what they call it on Venus, right? So let's honor this tradition with some small talk first. Please allow me to ask you a question—why… are you two… here alone? I'm ever so curious to hear your answer."

Both of our heroes did not reply, for the truth was best kept on the inside. Time passed.

"Well, I know why you're here alone…" Fleishman stood up, appealing to the crowd of guards and workers around him. His suit jacket flew through the air like the cape of a superhero. "You're here all alone because your scumbag skeleton has finally died or something. If the empire were thriving, there'd be more colony ships, and I know your boss's brain better than you do. If he really suspected disloyalty, on one of 'his' planets, he'd spare no taxpayer expense to go out and crush it. Sending two retards in a pod is proof that we can finally relax. Either your Tsar is dead, the empire is dead, or potentially and best of all"… He giggled his head from side to side as he spoke, "…they're both fuckin' dead!" The President turned to his men and bellowed loudly, "Mr. Ignatyev, get the finest spirits from our collection. Converter #3 always brews with subtle fruity hints a tinge of cider. Tonight we celebrate, boys!"

Fleischman stood up and began pacing back and forth over his "realm." "I thought one day they'd send an army to crush us, to turn us back into serfs for their exploitation, but it's over; you Muscovite trash are done. This is our planet forever; 'truth fucks lies,' and the truth is your emperor is dead; the tyrant is dead!" His men clapped and hooted with approval. He did a strange fist-pumping dance, then froze in position dramatically, like a kabuki actor. He then turned and approached #148. With each step, he could only look down on him less and less as he went down the steps before his throne. Getting to the bottom, he seemed like a twig next to a tree trunk.

"There is one tiny downside to this glorious revelation that you have brought to my attention. You know, it was always my dream to kill the Tsar myself for what he did to me. Even if he is just an AI in a chrome box, it would have still been fun to carve him… it… into pieces. But now, alas, I'll never get the chance."

"And what did he do to you?" Klyookva asked, popping out from behind #148.

"Well, you're both 'public servants.' You've been upgraded in some way. I don't know what your deal is, but hubby over here, I bet he can regrow horrible wounds like most of his battle brothers, right? Can you believe that, boys? Even without the fancy getup, you could put a bullet right in his chest and he'd probably get right back up in a few minutes. I'm sure he has some other doodads in him too, which do something cool, but can you imagine? This guy can come back from the dead! You could stake him like a vampire and he'd just pull it back out! Simply amazing! I don't know why the 'magic powers' they give you make you weigh so much but there must be a reason…"

#148 answered a rhetorical question with blunt facts, "I have a secondary metal endoskeleton as well as three times the muscle mass that I would otherwise have due to my internal converter running constantly at minimum."

President Fleischman looked perturbed at having his dazzling monologue interrupted, "Well, big boy, you settled my curiosity. But let me ask you this… What do you think I got implanted in me for putting up with a lifetime of your bullshit propaganda? What upgrade was I given to take this craft through the nightmare vacuum of space to this shithole planet from the captain's chair? Can you guess?"

"Oh, um, something for navigation?" Klyookva guessed like the know-it-all girl sitting in the front row at school.

"Well, my dear, that would have been just peachy—being able to directly link with the AI and navigate the ship as if it were my own body That is scientifically possible. That would even be 'cool.' As captain, I couldn't just sleep in those lovely pods, which means I was exposed to a lot of radiation and even more bone-and-muscle degeneration, floating around like a jackass in a sailor suit. If I had the magic box that's inside your husband, I'd be full of muscle too, with bones of iron. But no, no, they let my skeleton suffer all the way here… You see, the thing is, to become the captain of a star ship takes a ton of work, and for years of effort all I wanted was just a bit of a cybernetic reward from the state. Is that too much to ask?" His men quietly applauded like the crowd at a poetry reading. "But, as captain of a ship, going to a new planet, they chose to download into my brain… the entire library of… Russian fucking literature! Literature!"

Losing his arrogant demeanor, he got as close to #148 as he could, spitting in anger like a street dog.

They fucked my mind with Lermontov! The raped my spirit with Dostoyevsky! I can't even remember my mother's face but I sure as shit can quote every line from every book your black-smeared 'prophet' ever wrote." He struck a dramatic kabuki pose, turning his back to our heroes and began to recite:

> I loved you: perhaps my love has not yet
> completely died out in my soul.
> But don't let it bother you anymore.
> I don't want to upset you with anything.
>
> I loved you silently, hopelessly.
> Sometimes we are tormented by timidity,
> sometimes by jealousy.

I loved you so sincerely, so tenderly.
May God grant you to be loved by someone
else.

"And that is what your great 'Tsar' did for me, turned me into a library of culture so that nothing of *your* great 'Holy Russianness' would be lost as we built the colony. Not being able to calculate like a computer, live hundreds of years, or see other realities—they destined me to be a library of the shittiest and most backwards barbaric culture humanity has ever known." He looked at #148, pointing at him, staring down his finger as if down the barrel of a gun. "You guys could have made me an angel but no, you made me a portable hard drive, no no, a database of bullshit! And, do you really think I'll ever forgive you all for that?"

Chapter 8: Falling Back

Running up under a blue banner with white hand-painted letters that said "every man—a god," Fleischman panted with exhaustion from his maniacal monologue, still pointing at the chest of the Old-Timer. From next to his literal seat of authority, he began to speak, "You will leave this ship, get on your craft and go back to the subhuman hell from whence you came, *vatnik*, you backwards, ignorant troglodyte! You shall go or you shall die at my hands, for this is a planet of freedom, and equality is under our democratic law! There are no Tsars here!" His men roared with applause at the performance. Hoots and hollers echoed well off the metal walls.

The Ultra Heavy took a step forward, "Look, if you all change your mind and return to the good graces of the Tsar under the constitution and traditions of Holy Rus', I can make it so you, Mr. Fleischman, will be acting prince for a decade. The salary is 1,000 rubles per month and if you can win an election, then you can 'rule' even longer." Looking around the room, "And as for the rest of you, if you come back to Holy Rus', all will be forgiven, and I'll find something easy for you to do that pays 250 rubles a month. The work won't be labor-intensive and your pension will be similar in size."

His offer was met with nothing but laughter. Fleischman, returning to his throne to sit and enjoy the show, merely shrugged, hinting that nothing could be done to convince the boys to come back home.

The Old-Timer started up again, barking like a drill sergeant, staring directly at Mr. President, "So, you mean to say that you confirm that you are responsible for the planned vision for the first phase of the colony not coming to fruition AND that you are in a state of rebellion against the Tsar AND that you will not return to our empire under any circumstances AND finally that you refuse to negotiate? Are all of these statements *pravda*?"Delicately, President Fleischman placed his closed fist in front of his face. He raised his other arm and made a cranking motion in the air. As he "turned the crank," his middle finger went vertical. At this "witty" display of defiance, his men roared with laughter, some slapping their knees, others bracing themselves so as to not fall over.

#148, standing stoic as ever, replied clearly and concisely, "I don't care what you chose to do. I just needed to tick a checkbox. We're leaving." And with that he turned around and left through the open door, pulling his lady friend behind him. As he went out into the inner hull, the President bellowed one last line for the crescendo of his performance, "You're nothing here, boy! We are the rulers of this world!" The Old-Timer's spine cringed with disgust but he kept moving.

"What are you doing? Aren't you going to set him straight? You can't just leave and let him win like that," Klyookva said with maximum poutiness. Sighing, he replied, "And what exactly has he won?" She chirped an answer, "Well, he's acting like he owns us, like he's the boss. YOU're the boss and the Tsar's THE big boss." "Well, if you want to look at things in terms of winning and losing, today he won with words; tomorrow I'll win with bullets." She leaned her head to the side, "Oh, that makes a lot of sense!"

Having completely scanned the whole ship inside and out, and due to its simple layout, #148 knew exactly where he was going and exactly how he could violently return.

"Listen, I've been doing too much scanning, and too much digging today. I've completely burnt all the energy that could be converted from my stomach." His feminine comrade interrupted him, "So you're saying you're really hungry? Well, when we get back, I can make you some canned beef with buckwheat, my special recipe!"

"No!... that is kind of you to offer... but what I mean to say is—I'm out of juice. I can't scan anymore. I can't use my helm's omniscience till I get some fuel in the tank. I need YOU to keep your eyes and ears open. As soon as we leave this place, they may try to kill us." With those words, Klyookva's eyes went wide. "Oh!" she said, looking nervously around the room.

"Anyways... we are many kilometers from home and we've got a long walk ahead of us." They strode passed one of the orange delivery trucks as he said those words, wishing that it could be his. *300 years of service and I forgot to put a pack of* salo *on my belt today of all days; the one damn day it might actually matter. Lord forgive me for me stupidity!* he said within his thoughts. Klyookva didn't quite know what he was thinking but it felt bad and she hated when he, or anyone else, was hard on themselves.

After a few kilometers of dull linear marching over open steppe, our hero of the fairer sex started to hear a murmur in the distance. She looked over her shoulder and gazed at the horizon. Heading right for them was one of the orange trucks, kicking up dust as it went along. She was filled from head to toe with terror.

She grabbed his heavy and armored arm, yanking on it. "Look behind you!" she pleaded. He quickly complied.

"What are we going to do?"... "RUN!"... "But where to, there's nowhere to go, what if we...". "RUN THAT WAY!" he bellowed as he pointed in a random direction. His companion started to move but her short legs on a tiny frame were not to her benefit.

His instincts told him to pull his gun out and unload, but his brains wanted to take the truck "alive" as it was one hell of a resource on a barren planet that could be used later. He pretended to flee as he pulled off his mace from its magnetic sheath. The vehicle wiggled back and forth trying to go quickly over broken terrain. The driver, the guard who had mocked him earlier, had our man in his sights. His partner in the passenger seat tried to fire off some shots from the window but it was hopeless. The angle was terrible and the jittering of the vehicle was violent. As the driver neared his prey. he smashed down the gas pedal and smiled, assured that he'd put the *vatnik* in his place within seconds.

"Go with God" #148 said to himself as he pumped his legs to a stop. He pushed off, turning his body directly towards the speeding truck. With his frame low to the ground, and using perfect timing, he lept into the air punching through the glass of the windshield with his left gauntlet. This time, his knees didn't let him down. Gripping the body of the cabin of the automobile, he violently forced himself up and swung forward with his right hand holding the mace. The thrust happened in 1/30 of a second with the top spike of the head of the weapon detonating the skull of the driver. The elite-forged metal drove through his head as if it were as thick as a potato chip. The entire interior of the truck was blasted by gore, goo and bone chunks flying faster than the speed of sound. The guard in the passenger seat screamed in primal terror as he was bathed in human liquids. In instinctual response, he immediately projectile-vomited from horror, layering the vehicle in even more eldritch filth spewing in all directions. #148 shook the blood-soaked sailor hat from the head of his mace.

The truck was slowing down but the ride was getting bumpy with no one at the wheel. The terrified copilot of the craft opened his door, jumping out for dear life. He fell on the ground hard, gunless, and helpless to the forces of inertia, rolling like a puke-covered oil barrel down a hill.

The men in the back didn't know what was happening but they saw Klyookva in the distance running as the vehicle passed her. The two of them with assault rifles opened fire. Holding down the trigger, they desperately tried to keep her in their thrashing sights. The third, armed with a particle-beam cannon, was much more concerned with where the big target was. The sailor had about one good chance to take down the elephant and he didn't want to blow it. He became frustrated with his buddy's shitty shooting, bellowing out, "Quit wasting ammo on that fucking slut! Where's the heavy?" The answer he received was a boisterous, "What?"

#148, even without his helm scanning, could hear that they were shooting a lot and definitely not at him. The vehicle was losing speed quickly and the engine was sure to stall out when the RPMs got too low.

He sheathed his mace and swung from the vehicle, drawing his machine gun. He landed violently against the ground, rolling with the momentum. Quickly, he pushed himself up with one hand and burst forwards towards the box of the vehicle. Specifically aiming so the bullets would pass from one side to the other, without hitting any critical parts, he pulled down the trigger.

Doomf, doomf, doomf went the heavy machine gun rounds as the flares from the muzzle burst forth like the fires of hell. He swayed the barrel across the back of the truck as he continued to march, making sure that nothing could possibly survive. Ejected shell casings danced through the air to the rhythm of death being wrought.

Blood-curdling screams and bloody chunks of organs sprayed out from the back of the vehicle as the hail of lead continued to blaze through. Gritting his teeth, he kept the onslaught going, turning this delivery truck into a blender of human flesh.

After putting half a belt's worth of rounds through it, he marched towards the truck and stuck his gun barrel through one of the fresh openings—nothing was stirring, and not one body was still contiguous. Limping from yet another fresh knee trauma, from slamming into the ground as he fell from the then moving truck, our hero approached where he thought his female companion might be hiding among the crags and rocks of the local plains.

He found her not far away. She was lying on the dirty cold ground, crying. One of her legs had been blasted into chunks of metal and wiring. There was no blood, only gray industrial lubricants. There was something unusual about this Ministry of Ideology worker indeed.

Chapter 9: Two Cripples

Looking down on his fallen comrade, #148 spoke tactfully, "I know you've probably been asked this a thousand times, by every doctor, all your friends, and all your relatives and so on, but why weren't you able to just regrow your leg with restorative nanomachines? I think I've had like 4 sets of teeth regrown by this point." She continued to wail in sorrow but still answered, "It's because… I'm a fucking loser." Taking a deep breath, he asked very calmly, "Could you be more specific, in what exact way are you a fucking loser?" She laughed at his snide comment but continued ultimately to weep into her hands.

Her muffled words were hard to hear but she continued in her hysteria, "There's something wrong with me. Sometimes the nanomachines work, sometimes they don't. You don't know how many times I've tried to regrow that damn leg only for it to just rot and have to be ripped off again. Over and over again, they grow it, then they cut it back off! And do you want to know why I am in the ministry? Do you think it was my dream in life to be a cheerleader for the Tsar's ideas, then sleep in a shithole apartment alone my entire adult life? It's because I'm barren! I've never met a woman my age who doesn't have kids! They all do except for me! I am a freak who just happens to look really pretty. Well, I did look pretty when I was twenty and had two fucking legs! Do you know how many powerful men I've met being a showgirl at car and gun shows? They all fall in love with me until they find out that there's no leg in my boot and no buns coming out of my oven! Now that I'm getting old, they don't even try to trick me into having sex anymore. I'm invisible, and who wants to pay for a barren one-legged hag? WHO? Fucking no one, that's who!"Tilting his head and leaning into his words like a creaky door, #148 began a careful verbal maneuver: "W-e-l-l... I wouldn't say... no one wants you." She looked up at our helmed hero. From the ground, he seemed to tower over the sky itself. There was a gleam of hope in her eyes as she stared at the titan looming over her.

"Look, more of them might be coming. Let's get out of here. I am sorry you lost your leg. I am sorry it won't grow back. I am sorry you can't have kids, but you can cry about this at home, let's go...NOW!"

He grabbed her tiny waistline and picked her up like a bag of potatoes. All she could see was the ground bouncing around as #148 lurched towards the vehicle. He opened the passenger door and threw her inside like a contact football on a pitch option play. He slammed the door and went round to the driver's side.

Klyookva splashed into the biological cocktail that permeated the entire cabin of the vehicle. "Awww, what happened in here?" she screamed, holding her nose and continuing to cry. "Death and duty happened," he said as he started up the engine, putting the big beast into first gear. The gas tank was thankfully half full.

[Redaction: The journey to #148's ship was uneventful and has thus been omitted for brevity.]

Chapter 10: Homecoming

A few Earth days passed. While the lady of the spacecraft cleaned the inside of the truck, the patron was able to put together a makeshift cane out of superfluous piping from within the ship. It was not the type of present that girls dream of receiving from a man of power and status, but she could at least walk again, if quite slowly, and that was a lovely gift indeed.

As they worked, the long fortnight's worth of darkness consumed the landscape. It was unlikely that Fleischman or anyone else would make a move on them in the long darkness. Their camp should be invisible to his ship's computers, if he even knew how to use them properly, or any other form of detection. Even so, #148 was surely the only one who could see in the near pure darkness.

He had parked the truck under another camo cloak and lower than the ship so as to avoid detection—nothing stuck out on the horizon. All the information that had thus far been gathered was organized by the AI and sent back to Moscow. So far, sadly, there had been no reply, although there was confirmation that all the messages were received. Our hero found this frustrating but understandable. The busiest human being in the solar system couldn't be expected to jump at his every word, even if he was a man of power within Holy Rus' and this mission was supposedly of grave importance. The survival of our grand civilization was always paramount. #148 was sure that he'd eventually get an answer. From the console of the spacecraft, he turned to his companion.

"Thanks for washing my armor. The smell was really

starting to get to me, not so much the gore, but the puke," he said with stern clarity. Quietly and with a sorrowful voice, she replied, "Oh, well, thank you for taking the plates out yourself. I've never been good at that kind of thing. It hurts my fingers." Her hands were indeed quite small and frail.

She laid there on one of the mats in the ship, staring at the ceiling and holding her new metal cane like a baby. "I'm sorry Oldie, I just, this might sound stupid, but, um, I miss my fake leg. I miss my real leg even more." His eyes opened wide as he tried to provide an honest but polite response. For her, it was still strange to see him with nothing on his head. With no thick layer of metal between them, he was like a different person.

He replied, "Well, I can surely understand that. I am not sure how you expected this adventure to go, but I doubt you thought you'd lose your fake leg in the process." She kind of shrugged, "Well, if you want me to be honest, I wasn't expecting this to go anywhere. My life is basically over. I can't be mom. I'm too old to be a 'cheerleader' anymore for the Tsar. I'm tired, Oldie. I've got nothing left. Women can't own property and I can't get married. I've been living in a government apartment my whole adult life. Our empire is glorious, but my place is a dump. You might not believe this, but I like being here with you better. I'd rather die here than go back to that nightmare apartment ever again!" She slammed her tiny fist against the floor in disgust. It made a quiet thud against the metal.

The Old-Timer looked into her eyes from across their tiny living space, "Trust me, I know exactly where you are coming from, not so much about the apartment, but about… being at the end of the road… I don't know how many times human muscle and bone can be regenerated and slapped back together, but I know I'm reaching the limit." She leaned forward, "But what do you mean? I've seen you fight. You're one of the best!" "I was the best, a century ago. Now I just keep up appearances. I could never beat one of the younger Ultra Heavies and it's real easy to look tough killing untrained, unarmored normies." She looked puzzled, "Well then, why did you come here? Tell me." He shrugged, "You know the reason I came here…. was to die or at least fade away just like you wanted to… I've done everything. I'm the oldest Ultra Heavy. I have countless progeny, gone on great adventures; I've had it all. But this is the end of the road, because I don't have the knees to fight anymore and I refuse to rot away in a wheelchair. But why I came here doesn't matter. I am going to have to kill Fleischman to save this planet. He has over thirty guys left alive, some with anti-tank weapons. I'll kill his ass, that I'm sure of, but as for me… I'm as good as dead… maybe when I was younger, I could storm a ship like that. You know, go in one-on-thirty and win, but not now. I don't have the speed, and they've got the rockets."

Klyookva scooted closer to #148 on her hands with a perturbed expression on her face, "You're telling me you are planning to die and just leave me here, all alone?" #148 stared at the metal floor and spoke slowly in a fatherly manner, "I am telling you that Fleischman has to die. There is no negotiation strategy, and he has doomed this colony with his egotistical madness. But… woman… I'll tell you the truth: yes, I am most certainly fated to die in the process. This is my duty and this is how my story will end."

"Well, that ending kind of fucking sucks!" she said, pulling herself even closer and pleading, "But what about me? You get to go out in a blaze of macho glory, then what am I going to do? Collect cow turds for converters hopping on one leg?" #148 smirked, "Well, you are free to storm the ship with me on crutches. We can die from rocket launchers together. It'll be like *The Master and Margarita* but with a horrific and gory ending."

Her face turned red and she slapped our hero, "I want you to live! In fact, I think that I might love you!" Turning his head in disgust at the teenage emotions coming from an adult woman, he quipped, "I appreciate the kind words, but that doesn't save the Titan colony. I'm going in and whatever happens… happens. You'll live though, and that's good enough for me. My word is final." He turned his torso and then body towards his machine gun and started to drip some drops of oil here and there. He reached for the rag he usually used to clean it.

Klyookva, visibly angry, stared at him, pondering something in her mind, the pistons fired behind her eyes as she looked at him. She reached out… and for the first time put her bare hand onto the flesh of his body. #148 felt a warm pulse race through his entire self. His vision blurred as if everything around him and everything inside him rose a few degrees in temperature and was relieved of the burden of gravity. He remained there kneeling, looking at his machine gun as reality twisted around him. He felt more and more like he was somehow in bed on a warm soft mattress during the middle of summer. He could smell the tea with raspberry jam and hot buns coming from a table that did not exist. With no missions in sight, nothing to fight, he had not a care in the world. Nothing seemed to matter in the warm glow; all he wanted to do was enjoy the peaceful warmth he had not felt in decades.

"What's happening?" he asked as he slumped over his weapon as if he was shot by a tranquilizer dart. His female companion embraced him and rubbed the base of his skull with her fingers. For him it was like she was massaging the inside of his brain. She was gently and seemingly harmlessly rummaging through parts of his mind. He provided little resistance.

She could see the shadows of his soul and personality dance, but somewhere, there within him, was the desire to die. He was not lying or exaggerating when he told her that he was about to meet his end. She pushed further and further, searching from corner to corner, hearing whispers and reading the blurry visions in his brain. She searched for this iron desire to die, through memories of children, war, triumph, contact football, construction, sex with… other women… and the painful process of becoming an Ultra Heavy. It was all there, but at the core she encountered a black bar.

She found it and grabbed onto it. It was the part of the male mind most alien to her, it was at his core: his sense of duty. He wanted to die to escape this crushing weight of a duty he could no longer perform. The metal bar had become black in his mind, spreading disease to all other parts. All she had to do was shift his sense of duty to something else. She would polish it and repurpose it. He could be bound to a duty that would force him to live. Thankfully, on the periphery of his mind, there was a powerful and growing deep interest in her. "So that's what you need! I'll give you something to live for, my dear."

Keeping her hand within his mind, she moved around to be in front of our hero who was on his hands and knees. She lifted his battered face with her other hand and said, "I submit to you, my husband" Dazed and swaying back and forth, he could only respond, "Wait…. what?" She turned around and slid rear end first towards him so her back was against his chest. She moved up and down a bit with her one arm raised, still making contact with this mind.

She repeated, "I submit to you, my husband." Tiny Klyookva could feel the terrifying strength of his arms begin to wrap around her and his crushing weight press down on her. The corrosion in his mind began to drip off. His sense of duty had found a new purpose. It was not with her hand in his mind but her rear end rubbing against him that he had finally fully accepted the offer. She could see his thoughts and everything that he wanted to do to her, and the logic by which he would want to do it. He wanted to consume her body, and she was thrilled by the idea. "You're all mine now, Oldie!" she whispered.

[Redaction: There is no need to go into great detail about what happened next as it would be purposelessly lewd. Thus, it has been removed.]

Chapter 11: The Long Night

"Do you love me?" Klyookva said, peering over his chest like a bunny peeking out of its den as they lay together in the dim glowing light of his ship. The fortnight of darkness continued: Cold had set in outside, and they continued their quiet waiting game together. "Well?" she asked with only her eyes, brow and *kokoshnik* visible to him. He gave a very official sounding answer, "By tradition, they say the first kiss is 'bitter' and that love only grows with time and I hope that'll we'll have plenty of time to grow."

A smidge disappointed, she declared "that was a diplomatic answer, not a romantic one!" "Well, it is the only answer that you're getting, my dear," he retorted. She looked over the hills and valleys of the musculature of his chest with his huge arm wrapped around her. "You sure have a lot of scars. Do they hurt?" she asked as she rubbed her finger over a particularly nasty old gash. "Well, they designed the nanomachines inside me to keep me in the fight, not keep me pretty. Skin quality is the lowest-level priority, but no, none of these hurt per sa." She continued to peruse him with great interest.

The ship's computer made a pinging noise and the warning light next to the main screen slowly pulsed. He kissed her and then put a blanket over her body as he moved towards the screen. The AI's message ended with the statement: "As per your request, I am alerting you of a significant heat signature within 500 meters of this location." "Computer, please show this signature more closely," he commanded. It was three men, mounted on presumably horseback, switching to infrared, that became clear. Probably a friend, potentially a foe, but they did not need to somehow wander onto this ship's location. "What's going on?" she asked, scared and somewhat hiding under her blanket. #148 quickly started to slide all the plates back into position within his hauberk. He had done this many times over the years and was quiet and quick, but there were many, many plates to be reinstalled after a full cleaning. "It looks like it is the cowboys, but what do they want during the middle of the fortnight? That I don't know. Anyways, they don't need to be made aware of where this ship is located regardless." He continued to get his gear rounded up and in proper order. "Are you just going to leave me here?" she gasped. "Yes, but I'll keep you posted as to where I am. In theory, no one should be able to find you, especially in the darkness. I won't go far without you."

90 more seconds of shoving, clasping, and closing finally ended with him lacing up his boots and donning his helm. "I'm off," he said. He told the computer to dim the lights and partially open the ramp so he could slide out. "See you later," he said as he vanished into the cold darkness. She grasped the blanket close as he went into the infinite night. As the ramp began to close, he started making his way towards where the heat source of man and beast came from. However, he made a bit of an arc to get there so as to make it unclear as to where he came from.

The three grim men previously seen in plastic tarps had upgraded for the cold. They had modified clothing that looked suited for the long night-time weather. Through the thick clouds, the glowing blurry yellow ball of Saturn was at the heart of the night's sky. No stars could be seen through the soup, only the glow of the gas giant.

"This is a waste of time. We'll never find him," one of them said. "I don't want to wait for the next night cycle, and it's not like you have any work to do in the dark. Just think of this like a vacation." He rolled his entire head under his cowl, "Yeah, the perfect vacation, looking for a pumped up cyber freak killing machine in pitch blackness… fun times.” “Unless we restore some connection to the empire, then no one will be having much fun. We can't live like this forever. We need this guy.”

“Good evening gentlemen!” the harsh voice of the Ultra Heavy bellowed from the darkness. Two of the three horses hopped out of surprise. The riders settled them down. The grim man with his machine gun in hand stared at them, “Were you looking for me?” They seemed surprised by the question, “Uh… well… yeah, so look, we know you've confronted Fleischman and that he tried to kill you… the thing is… well… we want to help you get revenge… and if we don't get more supplies from Moscow, we're all straight fucked… there are some other people whom Fleischman really pissed off besides us that you don't know about. You went to one of the two functioning collective farms. Trust me, this made big news, but there was another collective farm…that's been forgotten about, so to say.”

The helm on #148's head seemed to lean with curiosity as he interrupted with a question. Steam from hot breath on a cold night came from under it as he spoke, “What do you mean by there 'was' another collective farm?” A different horseman spoke up, “Well, there were three in total put together as soon as Zhukov died; now there's only two. The one I'm talking about was headed up by a priest. He and Fleischman didn't see eye to eye on much.” Coldly, he replied with thick sarcasm, “Well, what a surprise indeed.” The horseman continued, “So, I don't know what happened but the priest and some of the others fled towards the caves down by the lake… I've run into him when the cows really go far out of bounds… we've kept this a trade secret between us. Fleischman is so sure the priest is dead that he never asked about him. It looks like you need allies, and we need Fleishman dead. If we take you to the priest, do you think you can get him and his men onboard?”

After a pause, #148 answered, speaking as clearly as

possible, "Yes, I am quite good at 'convincing people' to do the right thing, but let me tell you something… if this is a trap… all three of you are stone dead… it takes a lot to kill an Ultra Heavy and with my dying breath, I'll smoke you all if you betray me… you got it?" As he finished his words, the horses' eyes widened as if they somehow understood the threat. The lead cowboy answered in a soothing tone, "We… understand the price for treason… shall we head out?"

[Redacted: Some time passed.]

Back at the ship, the massive head and armored shoulders of #148 emerged from the opening ramp. His new bride was quietly looking at information on the ship's computer, nude. The colors of the screens and buttons reflected off of her chiseled but feminine physique. "Put your dancing shoes on, we're heading out," he said. "Oh! You're taking me with you?" she replied. "Well, we may be gone for a while, and I don't want any search parties to find you while I'm away. That is to say, I can't risk leaving you alone here. Suit up, we're taking the truck. I'll lock this place up and set the ship to hibernate while we're gone."

#148 relayed to the computer all the new information that he had regarding Titan's crisis and ordered it to be sent to the Throne. The AI successfully sent the data, but alas there were "no new messages." So far it looked like his words were not making it back to Moscow, or perhaps, he thought, maybe Moscow doesn't care.

[Note from the Tsar: Moscow does care. However, we do not have infinite resources.]

They left the ship, locked it up, got in the truck and drove off into the darkness with the cowboys.

Chapter 12: The Long Drive

The horseman and our heroes in the delivery truck slowly made their way over mostly flat terrain through the darkness of the two weeks of night. #148 took his eyes off the road for a moment. "What's with the bag?" he asked in reference to the large military sack between them on the bench seat of the vehicle. "Oh, I mean, I was sure you'd want to have a snack on your way back so I packed a few things from the ship!" This type of treatment was somewhat alien to our man after being alone for decades at this point. "Well… that is extremely caring of you… you make everything nicer somehow. The ship is pleasant. This truck is now pleasant… but, anyways, I brought something for you too. There's a civilian rifle behind the seat. If something goes wrong, you know what to do." She awkwardly leaned over to take the gun from behind the seat. It looked very small and simple compared to her husband's preferred firearm. She looked out towards the dim horizon, as she put the magazine in and racked the bolt. The outside was lit only by the headlights of the vehicle and the muddy reflection of Saturn beyond the clouds.

After many kilometers, the machine and equines arrived at a set of caves by the dark waters of a lake that stretched to the horizon. One of the horsemen went ahead and waved for our hero to stop his vehicle. He put it into park and turned off the engine. "Wait here," he said, grabbing his machine gun and hopping out of the cabin of the truck. Hitting the ground, he felt that sting of pain through his knees. No matter how many years in agony, he could never remember that he was too old to be jumping out of trucks.

He quietly winced in pain inside his helm, then, shaking his leg out, started to move towards the cliff and caves. One of the cowboys went up to the largest cave, the entrance to which was blocked by various plates of metal, probably taken from their former collective farm. There was no light from behind them; everything was dead silent. Looking forward, his helm projected into his brain a rough layout of the first few meters of the caves. There were objects of human usage, but no men to be seen. The draw distance was not so good due to the thick rock. However, he was getting signs of movement coming from somewhere else.

"Hey, Father Seraphim, open up, would ya?" one of the riders said impatiently, kicking the metal plates. Searching for the heat of human bodies wasn't working. He switched over to detect electrical signals and everything became quite clear.

#148 called out in a jocular tone, "Hey cowboys, I am going to lift my gun up in three seconds, and open fire at a target right above us. I want you to ride the hell out of here as soon as I pull the trigger, you got it?" "What the fuck are you talking…. ah…" The hint penetrated the thick winter garb over the rider's head. "Okay, boys, 3, 2, 1…"

And with that, our hero swung his gun up to his chin and aimed for the edge of the cliff right above himself, letting loose a volley of automatic fire, sweeping the gun's aim from left to right. Between the explosions, he could see the angular, animalistic-bodied drones. The robotic beasts began to move, jittering through the strobe light effect of the gun fire. The Ultra Heavy readjusted his aim and put two rounds through the nearest one. He clenched down on his internal clutch and set his converter to medium.

The horsemen hopped on their steeds and fled at full gallop as instructed. In the cabin of the truck, Klyookva heard the thunder and saw the flashing lights, but she was on the wrong side. She wanted to push herself across the seat but she had no leg to do it with. Frustrated, she gritted her teeth and let out a yelp, trying to think of what to do. After a long single second, she threw the civilian rifle onto the driver's seat and started to scoot across with her butt and hands to get into a better position.

The metallic creatures leapt from the tops of the cliffs down at the mighty cyborg. It was like a rain of corpses falling at terminal velocity towards him. As they fell, he could finally see the details. They were a pack of "sheep dogs" fresh off the assembly line—fully autonomous drones that moved and looked like large canines. They were the most basic combat and policing unit of the Fascists. Each was pathetic as an individual, but quite deadly in big packs, especially with the element of surprise, and in this instance, the high ground.

12.7 mm bullets ripped through another one of the manufactured monsters. #148 lifted his gun vertically with his left hand to block another diving drone. It deflected off his arm and shoulder armor. The other "dead" one he had just shot collapsed two meters away. He drew his mace from its magnetic sheath, lifting his right arm high in the air. After three centuries of service, he knew that when fighting dogs, never let them take you to the ground and always keep your weapon hand high above the fray. He clenched the muscle inside himself to put his internal converter to maximum. As it revved up, it felt like time slowed down. He could feel a blind rage of testosterone and adrenaline take over.

One of the dogs lunged from his left. He swatted it away with his gun. Another from the right and yet another from the front jumped at the same time. He swung his mace forwards, taking one down, but allowing another to clamp down on his leg. The impact of the mace hit directly on the metal skull of the sheep dog. Its cold steel jaws were slammed shut, while glass exploded from its single eye-camera. Having its head turned into a crumpled can, it fell over blinded and flailing. He raised his arm yet again to take a swing at the one that latched onto his right leg.

Not only were its teeth sharp but it was biting down with the pressure of an industrial vice. His armor was holding. His endo-skeleton was top of the line, but given time, its jaws could crush anything. As he swung his mace, more and more dogs lunged at him. He utterly smashed the torso of the biting beast gnawing his leg. Its battery exploded with corrosive juices; its spine of wiring was trashed. The metal mutt went limp but its jaws remained locked solid roughly around his ankle.

Klyookva looked on in horror as more and more steel canines lunged into battle. Her newly beloved was moving so fast, she could barely see what was going on in front of the truck's headlights. His mace swung wildly. Chomping metal biting sounds filled the cold night air. "Oh shit, what am I going to do?" she said, frantically trying to get a good aimed shot. The iron sights of the gun wiggled in front of her, never presenting a clear moment to shoot.

One of the remaining dogs bit onto his left gauntlet. Raising the dog and his gun above his head, he pounded down with the spiked pommel of his mace from the opposite hand. But the impact forced the bit down even stronger as the robots head was crushed into position. During the impact, another dove for his throat. He clenched his shoulder pad to his helm and punched it away with his arm holding his machine gun. The manufactured animal bounced along the ground only to quickly stand back up and rush forwards again.

Kylookva could do nothing. There was no shot to take. She didn't know what was worse: getting bitten or getting shot, but then she saw two more "dogs" appear in the glow of the headlights. One seemed defenseless but the other was larger than the rest, and on its back was some kind of energy weapon. *Oh, no,* she thought, her eyes went wide and she adjusted to shoot, resting her gun on the side mirror. The big dog braced to fire… Klyookva prayed for

God to make the rounds hit… and she pulled the trigger. The bullet whizzed, hitting its upper right leg, leaving a perfect impact hole and causing the critter to stumble. *It went right through!* she thought and kept pulling the trigger over and over. The angle was awkward. She had no leg to brace against but she had to make these shots count. *Boom, boom, boom,* she blazed through the whole ten-round magazine, leaving the specialist sheep dog floundering from the damage, kicking wildly in all directions from the ground. Blazing in from outside of her field of vision, #148 exploded forward, smashing it over and over again. His torso swung back and forth like the turret of a tank unleashing a combo of strikes, each crushing the metal exterior of the robot.

Klyookva reached behind the seat, slapped in another magazine frantically. "Oh gosh, what am I doing!" she yelled. Having slammed the bolt, she leaned back out the window, only to be greeted by a pale, blue, metallic dog jumping straight for her. She screamed as she unloaded the entire magazine into the darkness. God's graces must have shined on her as she soon heard the noise of the sheep dog slamming dead into the truck's door like a motionless wet sack of potatoes.

She fumbled and searched for more magazines, but just as her tiny gloved fingers made contact with another one, everything had gone silent. #148 had managed to finish off the rest, but she saw something that gave her deep concern: two of the now dead dogs were still clamped onto her husband. The one attached to his leg was dragged across the ground as he marched towards the final and seemingly unarmed robot. He flailed his left arm to free it but the robot's jaw was not budging despite having a completely snapped neck.

#148 scanned the final robot. Its extremely thin metal exterior hid zero secrets from him. This one was loaded up with communications devices, scanners, and transmitters—someone had been watching the fight. He could see that inside of its back there were two slots for hard drives and both were full. The Old-Timer took aim and with the greatest of care smashed its skull in with his mace. He sheathed his melee weapon, threw down his gun, and one-handed forced open the flap over the hard drive. The now headless robot was perfectly motionless as it was being dissected. He gently removed the hard drives. They were formatted for DoorWay OS, but he could physically send them back to Moscow one day for analysis. Picking up his gun, he walked over to the truck with dead dogs still clasped to him. "First off, decent shooting, and secondly, wrap this in something and put it in the glove box, so it doesn't break." As he handed her the hard drives, she said. still panicked, "Oh, okay!"

[Note from the Tsar: We cannot underscore the "creativity" employed by our eternal Fascist enemies who try to steal newly terraformed planets away from us. Yes, as part of the Smolensk Agreement, each of the great powers is entitled to at least 5% of each terraformed planet even if we have done all the work. But the Fascists will do anything to steal our resources. This pack of sheep dogs was probably part of a preliminary scouting mission to analyze what parts of Titan are the least defended and most valuable for them to acquire quickly before the planet settles mostly under the control of Holy Rus'. As they say, "It is far easier to take an unmanned trench." Sadly, Titan being successfully terraformed yet improperly colonized would lead to catastrophic problems later down the road, that is to say the dogs' analysis, if sent back home, would prove to be all too tempting of an offer and the Fascists would jump on it. My Heir, I apologize for the failures on Titan. I should not have completed a terraforming project during a time of great crisis. This single mistake has led to decades of chaos and problems.]

"Oh, Oldie, you know you've got robots stuck on you?" A deep sigh came from under his steaming helm, "I've noticed… I'm going to need your help… look around in the truck... are there any tools or anything?" "Oh, um, tools? Okay, let me look" She put her weapon down and whirled around, her rear end jostling back and forth in her tight suit as she searched. The view was very pleasant for our hero, but he needed to free himself, not fantasize. He went over to a rock and put the head of the dog attached to his left arm down onto it. He beat away at it like a blacksmith at an anvil, taking care not to hit himself with his own mace. With a few strikes, its grip let up and it fell off. "That's one down."

The problem was the one attached to his ankle was too far away to hit easily with his mace, and his unbending rusty knees wouldn't let him get close enough to really whack it. He tried a few practice swings but just couldn't get the angle. "Hey would this thing work?" his lady companion yelled through the night as she waved a crowbar back and forth out of the window. "That'll do. Hop on down here and help me." Klyookva opened the driver's side door and slid down. As her one leg hit the ground, she grabbed the cane that he had made for her. She slowly hobbled her way over. "Put it in its mouth. See that gap right there?" "Oh, okay, like this?" she chirped. "Yeah, now push down with all your body weight," he politely ordered. "Oh, do you think 45 kilograms will be enough?" He barked in reply, "Eh, don't overthink this; just do it!"

As she pushed down with all her weight and might, he began to kick its muzzle with his other leg. Once, twice, and thrice and their combined efforts did the job.

As the dog slipped off, Klyookva fell forward. The ground raced towards her face seemingly at the speed of light, but then a gloved hand wrapped itself around her head stopping her fall. He had caught her like a contact football in the back of the end zone. He held her whole body to his with one arm. She turned her head to look at him. "This is very romantic!" she said. He raised his helm, kissed her and said warmly but quietly, "I think so too."

His wife sat down more properly, moving off of the grip of his wide hand. "Why are we doing this?" she asked. "Is this really the time for philosophical questions?" he replied stunned and with slight annoyance. She ignored his response and, looking down at the ground, began to speak, "You guys, in the big armor, the Tsar tells you things, doesn't he? Things that the rest of us will never know." Pushing his helm back down into position, he stated clearly, "Only the Security Council and the Tsar himself know *istinoo*. However, we get bits and pieces, and within reason, I can say that I have theories about many things that happen within Holy Rus'." She turned to look at him and with a slightly annoyed face she asked like a child to her father, "Why did we terraform this planet? We did it, but we didn't send anyone here. Why are we fighting here for survival so far from the Sun? Why are we even doing this?"

#148 took a deep breath, "We need to keep moving… but I am pretty sure that ultimately everything we do is basically 'busy work' or some form of it." She looked as if she had seen a ghost, "What do you mean 'busy work'?" "If you think about it, once 3D chemistry and then the converters were invented, that ultimately ended man's struggle for survival. We could be living on just Earth, in paradise, in a new Garden of Eden. But, if we did, we would rot away. Man is only great when he is in a battle for survival. The Tsars of old sent us out to fight, to die, and colonize, simply so as to not rot away from the futility of a meaningless existence. Every terraformed planet and the insane expenditure in manpower and resources happens merely to keep us in a fight for survival. Do you really think we couldn't just exterminate all the Fascists or, hell, even the Southerners and just be done with this? God would forbid such a sickening action, but the existence of 'others' to fight with and compete against keeps our state machine running, and I should know; I am a machine of the state. Was that answer good enough?"

"Oh, um, yeah," she replied with massive disappointment as they both began to stand back up. "But, wait, if you know all this, why do you keep fighting, why risk your life for 'busy work'?" He tipped his helm up, hacked up phlegm and spit on the ground to clear his throat. "If I wasn't doing this, what the fuck else would I be doing, jacking off and playing video games?"

[Note from the Tsar: My Heir, although #148 is overall accurate in his statements, he was unable to see that which I believe must be pointed out to You for the survival of our Great Civilization. We are approaching a "crisis of "meaninglessness" much like those we survived during the 20th-21st and 30th centuries. Those were purely ideological in nature and perhaps part of a natural cycle, but this time there is a somewhat physical component to the approaching crisis. We've colonized the Galilean moons and Mars. The Moon, that is Earth's moon, cannot be altered as it is far too small. Mercury has proven to be unfit for human life after terraforming. And moving into Venus would require a genocide that God would never forgive. Titan is the last truly viable body in the solar system that we can integrate, that is to say, there's nothing left, nowhere else to expand. There is no other great mission for our people. Sending man beyond the solar system is only theoretical. Very soon we shall find that our people have nothing to sacrifice for, nothing to dream of, no great mission to push for, and this shall be our doom. The message of Christ that we should be grateful for what we have and in a Heideggerian sense be satisfied with "mere existence itself," that is to say, be content with a dasein of sorts can only last a century or two perhaps. I am not sure how long I will continue to exist, but

after We fully take control and bring Titan up to imperial standards, We... that is to say... You will have three or perhaps four generations to find a way out of this "dead end." I wish you the best of luck with the most difficult ideological challenge we have ever faced.]

Chapter 13: The Monastery

The cowboys made their return after things got quiet. The one of them with the raspiest voice spoke abruptly, slightly spooked as to what transpired, "Look man, this cave, the one in the middle that is all covered up, that used to be open, and that is where they used to live. If they're alive, they're in there somewhere." Through the vision of his helm, #148 could see where the bolt was keeping the door closed. He had no desire to simply smash though it, so he snuck his finger into one of the gaps, slowly turned the bolt and opened a small door. The mounted men hopped off their rides and tied them up to the inside of the door. The group of five began to go into the dark cave.

The walls were etched with crosses, prayers and symbols not entirely familiar. Although this planet was "new," the writing looked ancient, as if it had been written by the ancient Christians hiding in the catacombs of Rome before Constantine. Perhaps the residents found this just as inspiring as the Old-Timer did.

The cave seemed to stretch on and on, going deeper and deeper, all the while getting thinner. However, there was a slight smell of food and glints of light ahead of them. The materials in the thick rocks made the sensors of #148's helm become useless. One of the cowboys had a tiny digital lantern with him. Our hero put his lady's hand on his belt. "Grip my belt and follow me. I'll go slow." "Okay," she replied, fighting to keep balance with her cane going over broken terrain in near total darkness.

After some minutes, they came upon another makeshift door, from behind which light was gleaming. Above it in the dim light were written in fine script:

Proverbs 8:13:

> "The fear of the Lord is hatred of evil.
> Pride and arrogance and the way of evil and
> perverted speech I hate."

Gently pushing the door open, our hero calmly but loudly proclaimed, "We are not enemies. We come in peace. Don't shoot; we mean you…" Five extremely thin men sat around a table. They were picking away at tiny portions of what looked to be fish from rectangular wooden plates. Four of them were in the same type of bland clothing as all the colonists who didn't oppose Fleischman directly. But the one nearest to them, with a balding head and long black beard, wore the daily black garb of an Orthodox priest. Tied to his neck was a cross carved from wood of the tiny local trees.

It was the priest who rose briskly in reaction to visitors. "God Almighty be Praised, the Tsar has sent his finest; he has sent the Ultra Heavies! Praise be indeed!" #148 was forced to burst his bubble. Drawing out his words, he replied with a hint of sarcasm, "Well, He did send an Ultra Heavy, not the Ultra Heavies." For a brief second, there was a glaring stunned stare of disappointment on the priest's face. "But why are you alone?" he asked. Before getting an answer, he turned, "And Stepan, is that you too? I thought you were dead." Stepan, one of the cowboys, replied shrugging, "No, no, Father, I am still alive." "And the wife?" "Yeah, she's making do."

#148 approached the priest for his blessing. Klyookva, holding onto his belt was pulled along by default and the others followed. It had been so long since he had had guests that the crossing movements of the priest's arm were slightly out of sync as if he were giving blessings with an accent.

"We have very little to offer you. We survive on the fish and seaweed from the lake. The cave has mushrooms, and clean water condenses here. There is at present… nothing else, although it does make observing fasts a rather simple affair," he said smiling. The priest tried to add some brevity into their dire circumstances.

#148 responded, putting his hand on the priest's shoulder; it was like a bear gripping a soft beehive. "Father, I will take you up on your offer of food and drink, but we must talk now. I need information. What is this place? Why are you here? From what I understand, Fleischman cracked down on your collective farm, right? Tell me the whole story. I need to know everything that has happened on this colony. This is of vital state interest."

The priest took a deep breath inwards. His eyes looked to the side of his face, as he prepared for a big answer. "The landing went as planned. Everything seemed to be going fine until Zhukov died, and it became clear that no second ship was coming anytime soon. I can't say that things happened overnight, but very quickly Fleischman was able to ride the wave of this crisis. He said many things which at first were true and made sense. He would say, 'The Tsar is far; friends dear are near' or something like 'They've abandoned us, Titan is ours thus.' These catchy slogans made people have faith in him. They needed a leader and there were few to pick from. Basically, he said that the old way of doing things didn't apply here. How could we maintain the rules of a solar-system-wide empire with not even enough people to fill a small stadium? He filled us with a spirit of revolution, a spirit of change, all based on the raw *istinoo* of the situation. And with Zhukov being in the Kingdom of Heaven again, we needed a leader. And this is where I committed a great error, or perhaps I should say the greatest sin of my life."

"Hmmm, go on" said our hero.

"I committed THE greatest of sins. I saw evil rising.

I saw him twist the minds of our brothers and sisters and yet I did nothing. Fleischman quickly made it clear to everyone that somehow his control over every gun and every converter on the planet was somehow fair and that everything would be distributed 'equally.' I knew in my heart that would be untrue, but I allowed my conscious mind to lie to me, having 'faith' in his words. I knew this all and yet I did nothing. Fleischman has some kind of power over people, his words carry a weight like no other. I cannot describe it. His speech is otherworldly and demonic. I agreed to everything he said, even the most foolish and blasphemous statements. He could tell you that day is night and you would believe him outright. Satan truly stands beside him."

"This is similar to what others have said, but how did you end up here in this cave?"

"After it became clear that we were not citizens of Holy Rus' but slaves on collective plantations, only then did I begin to raise my voice. But his spies were everywhere. Most people just sort of went along with these lies. But a certain minority became his fanatics, hanging on his every word and whim. They, in their heart of hearts, shared his vision. Some of them must have informed him of our attempted 'subversion' of his grand plan for a land of total 'freedom and equality under a just authority by, for, and of the people.'"One day he came, not only with an entourage of his own men, who were the initial ship's crew, but with the residents of one of the other two collective farms. You must understand that, and I tell you this in front of God as my witness, the conditions on the farm were worse than our cave-monastery, and yet, the others, our own brothers, were told that if they drove us out, they could have all of our resources. With his rhetoric, he turned us into dogs fighting over rotting garbage to survive. He turned us against each other with greed for the pathetic scraps we had, all the while laughing from elegance in his ship."

"On that day when Fleischman arrived, he, with arms spread, screamed into a microphone, "Death to superstition" and "Every man—a god." Then he sent his crazed horde to kill us all. Many laid down to accept their fate. Some fought and died like true Christians, but we ran away. Perhaps God can forgive even cowardice as we were able to find this cave after what seemed like running for days into the wilderness. My whole adult life, I looked at the cross and knew that death for triumph is something expected out of all of us, especially priests, I didn't die for the Faith then, and I certainly deserve to now."

Klyookva chimed in, "You really shouldn't beat yourself up over this. I mean this monastery is quite nice to be honest. Well done!" This was correct. Somehow they were able to maintain a few digital lamps. Perhaps they had scavenged enough materials for places to sleep and sit. Food was stored in small plastic jugs. Looking up, the walls were entirely covered with makeshift icons and quotes of scripture. They had brought humaneness to a small pocket of an inhuman world. "Girl, all I can say is that I pray for forgiveness, and I try to think about things greater than my personal condition, but this proves to be... difficult."

#148 stepped in front of his newlywed wife to bring back the priest's attention to the deed at hand. Towering over him, he began to speak.

"There is not that much time until another long day approaches. At dawn, I plan to strike the vessel of Fleischman. I've come to this planet with arms, but not manpower. I need you and your..." Our hero was at a loss for words to describe the exact nature of this place and its residents... "fellow monks... to come with me during the assault. All I need is covering fire to get in without getting shot in the back. It'll be my job to go deep into the ship and kill Fleischman. From what I understand, he never leaves it."

Stepan jumped into the conversation, "That's true. He

doesn't leave anymore. I haven't seen him outside in ages, but it's not like there are many places to visit here though." #148 replied dramatically, side-stepping so as to face the cowboy, "And especially if he doesn't leave, I can probably close up the ship with him trapped inside of it. Regardless, the main thing is that I need you all to provide support fire as I make my advance. If I take the ship itself, this all ends. So are you in?" He finished his statement, stepping back to look directly at the priest and his compatriots. "We agree, but how are you so sure this will succeed?" asked the priest. "There are tendencies to these kinds of missions, Father," he replied.

"I must repent for my cowardice. We're with you, but for now let us eat, drink and pray together." The priest gestured for his guests to it around a crude but large table. The other monks began to gather what food and water they had.

The priest led them in prayer. They ate what they had; much was discussed.

At the end of the meal, Klyookva slyly asked the priest to formally marry her to #148. Both men agreed and the act was done.

[Redaction: Over the hours leading towards the dawn starting the next long day, all of those who agreed to the assault began armed training using the weapons from #148's ship. This training process has been removed as the information is not of a vital ideological nature.]

Chapter 14: The Last Hoorah

With just a few hours left till sunrise, #148 asked his female companion to take a stroll with him down by the river about a half of a kilometer away. For convenience, he carried her one-legged body most of the way under his arm like a bag of cement. When the river came into view, he stopped and set her down. He took off his helm, tossed it gently to the ground and held her by the shoulders. Looking into her eyes, he began to speak in a fatherly tone. He had bad news to tell her and it was as if he had to inform the kids that Grandfather Frost wasn't real.

"Look, we are heading out soon, and I have to tell you the truth. I am probably not going to make it back. In terms of raw math, we have eight guys to pin down the exterior of the ship. When I get inside, it might wind up being 20:1, 30:1 or, hell, even worse. I'm old; my knees don't work, but Fleischman has to die for the future of Holy Rus' on this planet. The Fascists are already scouting with their 'dogs.' That means we need to restore order now, before something changes the dynamic here. Fleischman doesn't realize that sitting on that tightly packed ship is like voluntarily lying down into his own grave. I definitely know where he is, thus I can definitely kill him, and definitely restore order."

Klyookva was visibly upset, her brow furled with disappointment. "What do you mean, eight guys? We have five monks, three cowboys and ME!" #148 came close to her, tilting his head like a drill sergeant. "You are staying here… if we lose, you'll have to shoot yourself because they'll torture, rape and kill you anyways, but if we win, you'll live for sure. The thing is… if you go with us to fight on one leg with no combat skill, there is a good chance you'll die for nothing. Sorry, sweetie, the math says you have a better chance at survival if you stay here."

"But I don't want to," she replied, pounding her cane on the ground. "Well, you are going to. My math trumps your feelings. I want to give you the best chance at survival. That's what real love means," he said. She started to whimper up and cry, "That's not love; that's macho bullshit." He smiled and replied after a shallow breath, "The Ultra Heavies are the living embodiment of macho bullshit… you are staying here." "But what if you die? What will I do? I don't want to be a widow!" Smiling, our hero gave his retort, "You women worry too much about problems that could potentially happen. Wait till I actually die, then fret about it. Don't sign my death certificate before you see the body, my dear."

She looked deep into his eyes, put her hand against his skull and said in a commanding way, "You will fight to live. You will fight so that you come back alive. You are my husband. This is YOUR DUTY." As she spoke, those words time seemed to melt for #148. He felt almost drunk, like his brain was being rewired from the inside. Although he was sure his death was neigh, her argument sounded very reasonable, almost like a great plan. "You have my word," he said, dazed by her intrusion into his consciousness. "I'll fight to survive. That sounds fair to both of us. Now before I go, there is one way in which you can assist me that I'd really appreciate." After saying these words, he began to kiss her neck and move behind her. He started to unzip her protective body suit. He pulled it down to reach into it from behind to enjoy feeling her chiseled tiny body. She certainly loved the feeling of being felt up by his powerful arms and she could tell that he was enjoying himself.

Klyookva pulled her body suit all the way down. Propping herself with one hand on her cane, she pulled open her butt cheek with the other while bending over, exposing all of her feminine gifts to his eyes. "You see, my beloved, if you come back alive, you'll get to enjoy this whenever you like, I promise!"

[Redaction: The details of what transpired here are not critical to the meaning of the story.]

Chapter 15: Loading Up

"Men, as we have talked about, when we get within a few hundred meters of the ship, I will bring the truck to a full stop. You will hop out two at a time, turn to your RIGHT, then turn RIGHT again to face the direction the truck is facing. At this point, run for the small ridge that overlooks the ship. They may already be shooting at you but you must get to the ridge. Go prone, and begin laying down fire. Each of you has an army grade helmet and cuirass. As long as you stay down low, it will protect you. Keep your gaps closed and expose nothing but your face to shoot. Don't waste your ammo, take aimed shots, and most of all, don't shoot me in the back as I make my way in." #148 began to put on a demonstration. "And please remember to move to your right, push off with your left leg; if you twist your ankle, you're as good as dead, understood?"

The raspy-voiced cowboy replied, "Exactly, sir!"

#148 again demonstrated how to push with one's outside leg to turn 90° in the opposite direction. For some reason, this simple idea took years to learn for those who never played contact football in school. He had tried to instill as much combat knowledge as he could into his militia, but the clock was ticking. They'd have to go in basically untrained. Thankfully all he needed was a distraction, and any idiot can shoot. All they had to do was go prone and shoot, that's it.

"Alright men, load up." And with that, all of the men got into the back of the truck. #148 walked towards Klyookva and said with frozen, resolute words, "I'll be back."

#148 turned from her and went to the vehicle. He took the driver's seat. as the sun finally began to glow through the goopy sky on the horizon. He performed the sign of the cross and put the truck into first gear and thus they began their one-way journey. Klyookva stood with the horses that were left behind, looking at the faces of the men in the back of the truck that she barely knew. They were crestfallen, knowing what could await them, and yet they went anyways. As men, this was their destiny. And as a woman, it was her destiny to wait at the home front.

The men in the back of the truck stared in silence at each other, none of their armor fit properly on their underfed frames. Not one of them looked or felt like a proper soldier, but something had to be done. They couldn't live as the servants or slaves of a madman. Militiamen didn't live long but they died with dignity.

Chapter 16: The Assault at Dawn

Our hero peered over the steering wheel of the delivery truck as his head sagged downward. Reflecting off his visor was the colony ship on the horizon. As always, the drop ramp leading to the outer hull was lazily down, as if it were inviting an assault. #148 had eaten to his limit as he'd need to keep his internal converter fed with energy during this suicide run. He clinched the muscle inside himself to push down his clutch and set the conversion rate to a medium flow. Immediately he felt the difference. As soon as it finished shifting gear, everything was visible. The data from his helm became as native as the sensory organs of his own body. Whenever his converter was firing, he became one with all the omniscient data his helm could provide.

Soon they would arrive and he would have to cut a path of blood into at least the inner hull, tearing out the wired explosives that he had noticed during his visit to offer Fleischman an olive branch. Thankfully, that visit gave him time to scan and record a full map of the vessel as well. Now the only thing that could destroy his plans was if someone actually altered the security pass system. He took a moment to pray to God that this had not happened and to forgive him for what he had to do: none of Fleischman's men could be allowed to remain on the ship alive. Mercy can often be punished by being shot in the spine—in all likelihood no one he encountered in the ship could be left alive. Furthermore, there were no nanomachine clinics to patch the wounded back up. Better to kill out right than make them suffer a long torturous death from infection or worse.

The orange truck finally rolled up to the ridge some 200 meters from the ship. The Old-Timer could see through the driver's side mirror that his crew of militia misfits were at least going in the right direction, stumbling and fumbling over the rocks, hauling gear they were not trained to be using effectively. As the monks and cowboys got to the ridge, the first gunshots could be heard. A bullet or two whizzed past the truck. #148 put it into gear and started to build up speed, going forward down a readily used path. Black exhaust belched from the machine as it drove forward.

Stepan made it to the ridge first. A rifle round pinged off of his shoulder pad, knocking him to the ground. He scurried to fix his helmet and actually bring his civilian rifle up to fire. He could see one of the men in blue uniforms out in the open firing at him. Scurrying around him were plenty of helpless locals just putting in another day on the job, till the gunfire started. More bullets flew by. Stepan raised his weapon, pulled the trigger, once, twice, thrice… every shot missing. The others got into position and started firing as well. Rifle fire cracked as finally a round went into the thigh of the guard. He went down to one knee, only to be shot two more times directly through the chest. The priest called out, "Brothers, keep your eyes open, fire at anything that moves!"

The truck barreled forward. From behind some shipping containers came more gunfire. Two rounds plinked around the cabin, accomplishing nothing. He shifted into a lower gear to power his way up the drop ramp, bellowing dark smoke from the exhaust filling the outer hull with a toxic fog.

"To the left by the containers!" cried Stepan to the others. They all adjusted fire on the big metal boxes. They could see one man dart away from the ship and into the open steppe, seemingly trying to make a run for it, having given up. Then another slid down the ramp to get out of the toxic cloud and ran behind some barrels for cover.

The truck smashed into all sorts of priceless equipment as it made its way to the end of the outer hull, parting the seas of enemy sailors in the long storage hall. The brakes screeched as #148 pulled right up to the door. His helm's scan showed off two men hiding behind another container in awe at what was happening. He pulled up the parking brake and grabbed his machine gun. Leaning out of the window, he took a bullet to the helm and another onto his chest. Armor saves made, he opened fire with his 12.7 mm machine gun. Inside the metal chamber of the outer hull, the echo was immense, bass-filled explosions filled the air as if God's wrath had finally come to end mankind. Sweeping from one crewman to the next, the rounds all hit their mark, causing rib cages to explode in every direction. Chunks of bone flew through the sky like a fireworks display of murder. All that remained were red stains and four detached legs in a pile.

#148 killed the engine and got down. He immediately cut the suspicious wires linked to the explosives all over the ship. There was a chance that this would set off all the bombs, if wired improperly. He took a deep breath, said a prayer in his mind, and pulled at the wires…

…Two long seconds passed and…

… nothing happened. It worked. At least the outer hull couldn't explode. He wove his gauntlet over the panel to accept security cards… the door quickly opened… "Total access granted to elite-level imperial personnel," the screen displayed. Another blessing!

The upcoming corridors were very tight. He drew his mace from its magnetic sheath and held his gun vertically to parry. Around the corner, he could detect two bodies. He went through the door quickly and stomped his right foot down to make a 45° rush to the left. His mace came down with full force on the head of a female crew member in service to Fleischman. Her skull exploded like a grape hit by a sledgehammer, sending hair chunks and goo flying across the room. Following through after the impact, he hit the other crewman with a right hook just as he was raising his rifle. He got off two shots that deflected off the side of his *troika* steel-plated hauberk. #148 could feel the giggling and wiggling of the metal as it dampened the impact. The man's head was spun completely around and he collapsed to the ground like a marionette with cut strings. He marched on.

Things were getting serious, #148 set his internal converter to maximum output. He kept moving through the corridors on the hunt. When he got to engineering, he could see that the most talented crew had locked themselves inside. All they could see was the bronze-gold helm of a terrifying predator looking through the porthole at them. They were like children trapped in a cage with a rabid tiger. #148 wove his hand over the pass-card system. He screamed in an enraged bellowing howl, "Computer, set engine room doors to remain locked on my authorization, Ultra Heavy #184 —227 990." He quickly moved on. With every second, the advantage of surprise and chaos was being lost. The pass-card display then read: "engine room permanently locked."

Next came another door. He ripped out the wiring for the explosives again with ease and made his way into the most dangerous part of the ship: the fuel reserves. One explosion here could bring down the whole damn ship, leaving a crater in its place. He sensed movement around the corner.

As they came into range of his helm's omnipresent senses, he could see they were setting up a machine gun nest haphazardly... a machine gun right opposite of the fuel tanks! #148 ran as fast as he could to close the 10-meter gap, his legs pumping like a pro contact footballer on a blitz. He clinched his teeth and screamed from the burning in his legs. Then all of a sudden...

His left knee gave out.

The signal from his brain to his leg cut out for just a fraction of a second. The titan thus was falling forward at full speed. He screamed in pain while the machine gun crew screamed in terror. His body skid along the floor smashing into them like a bowling ball striking pins. One of them took the brunt of the hit and was instantly crushed to death as their bodies slammed into the metal wall. #148 rolled to his right to bash one of the downed men with his mace. Automatic gunfire ripped through the ship as our hero could feel impact after impact hitting his armor and two biting right through to the back of his leg. He turned swinging wildly, impacting the arm of the crewman, shooting turning it into mush. He screamed looking at the remains of his limb at which moment he was silenced forever. #148 threw down his gun and pulled the man to the ground by his clothing, smashing his skull in with a full-force headbutt.

All of those shots hit; none went astray; nothing exploded.

#148 tried to gather himself, but age and fatigue were setting in. He again pulled out the wires to the explosives from one knee. His helm indicated that his nanomachines were working but one of the bullets was deep inside of him. Standing back up was agony. He angrily picked up his gun, gathered himself and opened the security door to get into the inner hull. The door opened and a mist filled the air. It blurred the info from his helm. #148 stumbled forward, finally swiping his way into the crew quarters.

And with that, he heard words in an all-too-familiar voice, "Not so fast, my friend!"

Chapter 17: The Standoff

"And this is the part of the story, where our hero has to realize that he has lost… did you really think that I'd be unprepared to deal with one of the 'servants' of our glorious metal skeleton?" the cold cocky voice of President Fleischman resonated throughout the cathedral-like hall.

#148 moved through the doorway to find the room was far from empty. It was unclear what the vapor was and there was no time for analysis. But what was clear was that there were plenty of men with heavy weapons aimed directly at him from the upper level. Fleischman stood in the pose of a Roman emperor a meter and a half in front of his makeshift throne. His blue suit framed his blue banner and its motto that hung above the fancy chair: "every man—a god."

Each side stared at the other in an endless moment of silence.

Fleischman, with obvious annoyance on his face, continued his monologue, "Let me ask you a question, big boy… what do you get out of all this… is the old dead man paying you that much? If this is about the money, perhaps we should have negotiated instead of you killing my very limited number of workers. You see, it's hard to find good help on a planet with a couple hundred people on it. Then again, for YOU, this is probably a moment of triumph! You've killed a few PERCENTAGE POINTS of the freedom-loving people of an entire planet… you are an elite-level *vatnik*, sir! It's a new tyrannical record!"

"It's not about the money. 3,000 years ago, our ancestors chose to create a civilization. Prince Vladimir embraced the message of Christ and we owe all those that came before us, and after him, including all the peoples who share in our cultural destiny, to continue that mission. If they had given up, we wouldn't be here. We… I owe them everything."

The President of Titan shrugged, "You see… this is your problem. Despite your physical power, you absolutely refuse to admit that you have the inherent mindset of a slave, you foolish *sovok*. You are fighting me, because you owe dead people? Look, around my friend. There is no debt to anyone, except for the invisible chains in your mind! You… are the exact reason why this 'Holy Rus'' needs to be finally done away with. You have the power of Hercules and yet you want to throw that all away because you owe it to dead ancestors you never met, who were probably the same type of drunk dimwits as the schmucks on the street today. And your loyalty to that dead Jew on a stick is something you Russians should have ultimately done away with in the 20th century… but you just couldn't do it. You couldn't live free of self-repressing magical bullshit, so you jumped right back on the Jesus express to fantasy land… TWICE NOW!"

As Fleishman rattled on, nothing moved even a millimeter within the large metal hall. Each man seething with adrenaline filled blood in his veins pointed his rifle at our hero.

"You see… your 'Tsar,' and the ones before him, and the presidents, and the general secretaries, century upon century convince YOU to sacrifice everything for THEM! That's the game, that's the grift, that's the con, baby, and I… that is WE are done being the type of sucker that YOU are. Here the strong go up, and the weak… mop up. As your God intended… well definitely as the Hindu gods intended for sure!"

"But anyways, so tell me this, *vatnik*, what have you gotten for thirty some centuries of slavery?"

Nearly instantly, #148 replied sternly, "A stable

interplanetary empire that provides prosperity for all and guarantees the survival of our culture into the future." Fleischman raised his finger quickly and wagged it back and forth, "But, my friend, that empire only belongs to the chrome king on his golden toilet seat." He took a few paces and threw open his arms and spoke in the tone of quotation…

> To be yourself in a world that is constantly
> trying to make you something else is the
> greatest accomplishment.

"You should heed the words of your black-smeared prophetic poet! But you, my friend… do the opposite. You wash away yourself into this 'civilization,' wasting all your potential. Your service is your own slavery. It is your addiction, for if you were to stop and think and look at your actions, you would see they have never served YOUR interests."

As Fleischman tried to seemingly manipulate his way out of this situation, #148 could feel that he was trying to pierce into his mind. He knew that feeling when some kind of entity wanted to take control. The invisible fingers of a demon were picking the lock to get into his skull. His vision was blurring; his spine started to tingle. Every word came slower and slower as time dilated around him. He needed to not concentrate on this rat's verbal vomit.

Staring with his physical eyes at the banner behind the President hanging from the upper level, his helm could see that there were a total of eleven crewmen with weapons on them. The problem was that four had rockets. He could take a lot of rifle fire; his armor would hold; his nanomachines could fix any wounds, but a direct rocket hit or four—meant death.

Fleischman's face turned red, "Are you even listening to what I'm saying?" #148's grim voice responded with a smidge of snark, "What would be the point? Neither of us can convince the other." The leader of Titan spun around and stood on his throne, grabbing a black device from within the pocket of his suit. Our hero allowed all this to happen, keeping his gun perfectly fixed over the base of the neck of his adversary but not looking into his demonic eyes.

"This device is my victory over your Tsar—my vital signs are linked to this ship. If you pull that trigger... and I die... then this entire thing blows." He made the noise of an explosion with his mouth, moving his arms in the silhouette of a mushroom cloud.

"That's right. All the food, all the converters, all the guns and all the talented people on this ship will be gone forever. If I die, then human existence on Titan dies with me! You get it? And if you were relying on standing near that major fuel pipe to save you from my men's rockets, well, I'm willing to risk it, my friend, and so are they," he said, tilting his head like a cute puppy.

"You see, you came here and never had a chance to win. From the very moment you began your crusade against me, you had already lost. Because unlike you... I believe in real ideas and not servitude."

"Live free or die!"

"I will either live free on Titan, or we will all die in this room together, but either way I WIN... and YOU LOSE.... you orcish enslaved cybernetic shitbag!"

#148 had precalculated how the swing of his machine gun would have to go from Fleischman across to all the crewmen with rocket launchers, firing on full auto. There was simply no way to do it in under 1.5 seconds, even with his internal converter pumping on maximum and perfectly timing the rate of fire. Untrained dimwits have a reaction speed of 0.3 or 0.4 seconds. Someone would definitely get a shot off—if they didn't panic and run away. During these moments of contemplation, the whimsical individualist continued his rant. His face was turning red and he began to spit as he talked like a diseased street dog.

"But now you can clearly see that you've lost! I know your Russian bullshit better than you do. They uploaded it into my brain, and in life or in death Titan shall be mine. I was destined to break our people free. Only once in a generation, a Solzhenitsyn appears who sees through your invisible shackles of lies! I will never go to your mental gulag… I am the liberator… and on Titan… I am a GOD!"

And standing like a statue of a triumphant gladiator, in 1/60 of one second after those words had been spoken—he pulled the trigger.

The first explosion from inside the chamber of his machine gun sent its devastating round right into the clavicle of Fleishman. From #148's perspective, the upper half of his body bloomed like a bloody flower separating into petals of gore and bone. He pushed his gun towards the first "rocket man," allowing the second round to shoot into nothingness as he swung. The third round chambered and fired on time. None of the crewmen had armor, neither modern, obsolete or otherwise. The heavy bullet hit his shoulder, slaying him in one impact like the slice of a samurai.

As he turned to the second "specialist," he detected the first signs of retaliation. The fourth round went into the darkness as he pushed the barrel, blasting towards the second rocket man of the group. His launcher still near his chest, the 5th machine-gun round caused the warhead to explode on impact. The crewman was turned into a fountain of guts, brains and blood spraying in all directions from the point-blank explosion.

At this moment, our hero felt the first impact of rifle fire. Two shots bounced off his left shin; another burst hit his left arm, ruining the swing of his gun. Another banged him on the head. His helm recorded and displayed each impact as "successfully saved." His sixth and seventh shots went into the darkness along the way but shot number eight which should have impacted the penultimate rocket troop went astray as he was being peppered by gunfire.

He tried to readjust as his whole body was being slapped by rifle bullets from various directions. The ninth shot missed, the tenth missed, the eleventh, however, found its mark, but it was too late. Within the tornado of ammunition flew two rockets at supersonic speed. His helm sensed them and one of the compartments of his hauberk exploded automatically in a burst of flak, taking out the first one in a brilliant glare of white light and shrapnel right at the two-meter mark… but the second made in through entirely.

His helm projected the warhead to hit him directly at the right base of his neck.

Although the rocket was fated to hit—it did not.

In that moment, the system recognized Fleischman's death. From each and every wall came an explosion. The ship had truly been thoroughly rigged to blow. #148 had cut the wires up to this point, and the engine and fuel were safe, but the crew chambers and bridge were doomed and he and the ship's crew in them with it.

From every wall and every surface came explosions. Metal flew through the air in such great quantities that it became a gray mist of doom. A furious rain of body parts danced through the air of the chamber as the explosions continued. A completely limbless torso spun through the air like a *shuriken* right before #148's eyes.

Rifle rounds, rocket warheads and now a seemingly endless wave of explosives battered our hero. His helm was in a panic to recognize all the impacts, some piercing, some not, some potentially lethal, some not. It tried to list them all but the sheer quantity of hits spammed the system to a halt.

Out of pure instinct, #148 continued to fire, blinded by the storm of information in his mind and explosions against his body. His final instinct was to just keep shooting. Even if you go down—keep the fire going… stay vertical… keep shooting… round after round exploded forth… but with the end of his belt… and a final "click"… he was embraced by only silent darkness.

The body of the Old-Timer lay face down on the metal floor of the ship in a hellscape of gore and fire. Everything had gone quiet; nothing moved but a few dancing flames. Every wall and surface was covered with blood and entrails. His mission was finally over.

Chapter 18: What Happened Outside?

Outside on the ridge, things for the cowboys and monks had gone rather well. After a lot of awkward gunfire, only one of the monks stopped moving. On the others there were bruises from impacts against the armor but these were of little concern. The enemy, under a rain of suppressive gunfire, was simply unable to hit them properly at that distance. Losing only one man in an assault was a fantastic result, but with adrenaline in their veins and their guns still trained on the outer hull and its surroundings, most didn't even notice that one of them would never return home.

When they heard the huge series of explosions from within the ship, presumably to them set off by the actions of #148, the cowboys cried to flee! "The whole damn thing's gonna blow; we gotta get the fuck outta here!" Stepan screamed at the top of his lungs, raising up to one knee and loading in another magazine.

As the whole vessel seemed sure to explode, the remnants of Fleischman's crew ran empty-handed into the morning light. Our militiamen stood up, emptying out their magazines at the panicked crewmen before turning to run as fast as they could. "The whole thing's gonna blow… run!" They tried with all their might to just put distance between themselves and the ship before it went off. Hearts pounding and legs pumping, they flew towards the horizon.

Running in armor with a gun takes great physical conditioning—something that the remaining monks lacked. The priest, noticing that one of them would remain on that ridge for eternity, said a quick prayer for his fallen friend with eyes closed. One of the cowboys took his gun from him to lighten the load. "I'll take that Father! Come on, we gotta move!"

They didn't know how big the explosion of a colony ship could be but it was sure to be terrible. This had been a victory for them with only one casualty. Fleischman was toast and the Titan colony would return to the loving embrace of the Tsar and Holy Rus' forever.

They ran until ultimately they collapsed into a ditch some two kilometers away. There they waited.

Chapter 19: His Helm

Seven hours passed in perfect silence and darkness within the inner hull. Now, not even flames lit the room. All that remained were droplets of light coming from the occasional sparks of exposed wiring and a few glitching computer panels.

It was a primordial nothingness.

At some point, slowly, #148's eyes began to open… inside his helm there was nothing. No information in his mind, no readout layered before his eyes. There was nothing, a pure black infinite abyss. He lay face down on the metal floor and agonizingly with his right arm detached the cable from his neck that connected the device to its fuel source: the internal converter near his stomach via his neck. Centimeter by centimeter, he moved his arm to his head and pulled it off with one brisk tug. The helm rolled across the floor like a head fresh off the guillotine.

He pushed his gauntlet against the ground to activate its small screen. Even this basic task caused true agony. The light in pure darkness glistened off his prized piece of protection that had come to a stop some 90 cm away from him. The helm's systems had been breached—its processors were trashed beyond repair. To crack his head gear like that, being made out of the most expensive and elite *troika* bronze in existence, requires an impact so powerful that no one should have survived it. No physical brains should be able to survive the death of the digital brains inside the device—and yet, he breathed.

For 300 years of service, he had worn that sallet of sorts. It had been with him across the solar system, in peace and in war, in triumph and in failure. All of his children had held it. It sat on his mantle in every family photo, but now it was just lifeless metal that had fulfilled its duty. Its service was over.

#148 could feel the nanomachines in his body working, and an insane hunger in his now completely empty stomach. The internal converter must have drained every molecule of fat it could find to fuel his restoration. He slowly reached for some concentrated *salo* cubes that he often kept in one of the various pouches on his belt. He pulled open the compartment, grabbed a few and smashed them into his mouth with burning pain as he swung his arm. He chewed, swallowed, repeated a few times and then waited, for there were no other options. Lying in a pool of sanguine liquid and body parts unable to stand—he had nothing but time to think.

Chapter 20: You Can Never Go Home Again

Klyookva sat upon a bench just outside of #148's ship. In this short time, she had begun to see it as the only real home she has had since leaving her father's care at 16. She began to ponder if somehow they could just live in the ship, or maybe attach it to a proper house somehow, "Oldie" should surely know how to install a toilet. But none of these daydreams could possibly come true if she were to again find herself all alone. She'll surely be in solitude for the rest of her life.

The day was the warmest she had experience here on Titan—it must have been a good 28°C. She tried to enjoy this summer vacation of sorts as she waited for what seemed like an unending eternity for our hero to return. With nothing but time, she cleaned, rearranged the ship and unpacked all the various crates and containers to see what was in them.

The piles upon piles of civilian rifle magazines were not so interesting, but she did find her old man's contact football *kosovorotka* that he had brought along for the ride. She assumed he played when he was younger or was just a big fan of Moscow's team. The jersey was so big that she tied a belt around herself and it basically became a dress that went down to her knees. The material felt comfortable, and it ever so slightly smelled of his body.

After many, many hours, she had cleaned everything twice, organized everything thrice, and Klyookva was beginning to fear the worst: that he had failed. Our heroine was on the brink of happiness, but perhaps it would all be for naught. She convinced the most powerful man on the planet to be her husband. A man who wasn't at all bothered by her age, inability to bear children, or stump where an elegant leg should be. Finally, there was someone to care for, who would protect her in return and give her everything. But it all seemed like a dream that she was waking up from. The reality of the situation at that moment looked to be quite ugly indeed.

Wearing his clothing and smelling his scents coming from them, she sat on a bench that he had whipped up for her, leaning on the cane that he had also slapped together when her artificial leg broke forever. They were here for such a short time and yet he became her world and everything reminded her of him.

She was reading a book that she found on the ship when she saw smoke and dust on the horizon. *Is it Fleischman's men?* she thought to herself. She floundered to go grab the civilian rifle that she propped up against the entry ramp to make a final stand. As she waddled towards it. she looked over her shoulder in panic.

Coming over the horizon came the heavily damaged orange truck that she knew so well, and behind the wheel was a man of great size in a dark set of armor, bearded with short white hair. From behind a layer of blood and filth, his eyes seemed to glow white.

She hobbled forward, smiling with unfettered joy, leaving the weapon at rest. The truck with lots of fresh battle damage drove up, halted, and #148 with his head bloody and bare turned off the motor. He slapped open the door, which now swung crookedly. He leaned out of the driver's seat and fell to the ground like a bag of concrete.

She moved towards him as fast as she could. She could see that his entire uniform and face, from head to toe, were soaked in blood. Some of the segments of his hauberk had been blown out, and dents and tears abounded across his gear. From behind his gore and grease-soaked mug she could see life in his pale eyes. He breathed in a single breath… and spoke…

"Well, did ya miss me, ya one-legged bitch?"

Klyookva rolled her eyes and gently slapped him, "Now, this isn't the time for jokes! You've been blown up!" Smiling and laughing, he replied, "They did more than blow me up… now, could you help me get this off? I'm having trouble standing." She looked with her bright, wide, naïve eyes and spoke in quick response, "Oh, yes, let's do that!"

She very carefully started to remove the plates from his hauberk when a dinging notification sound came from within the ship. "Klyookichka, could you get this one for me?… thanks… you're the best, baby," #148 said as he let his head drop back to lie flat on his spine. He groaned from the internal damage that remained and the unpleasant feeling of it being fixed by microscopic machines from within.

His wife made her way into the ship to look at the main display. She took a few moments to carefully read what was written. He could see that she was sort of reading to herself as she pointed at the screen with her elegant index finger. She sat with her legs crossed, which was always cute as half of one was absent.

"Honey… issue number one is… that you're dead." The Old-Timer lifted his eyebrows and shot back, "Well, I certainly feel pretty dead." "No, no, I mean they sent a copy of your death certificate and they really picked a good photo of you! But issue number two is… that they also sent a digital passport for a man who looks exactly like you, also weighs 250 kilos and has pale eyes… It looks like they've given you a new identity…" She reacted in disgust to what she was about to read, "And your new name is… Ivan Ivanovich Ivanov… ugh, yuck!"

#148 shook his head on the ground, "What creative

bureaucratic geniuses came up with that one? That's terrible, but at least it'll be easy to remember my initials – I...I...I... I am highly disappointed with this name!"

"Wait, wait, it looks like there is a death certificate and new passport for me too! It's being downloaded right now! And you, as in the #148 version of you, who is officially 'dead,' has been awarded the Hero of Holy Rus' medal for your assault on the colony ship, in which you 'died in an explosion,' saving the lives of hundreds."

Looking puzzled, he asked from flat on his back, "How the hell did they find out about that?" Klyookva raised her hand like a girl in elementary school and proclaimed, "Oh, well, while you were gone, I had nothing but time, so I sent a lot of messages in great detail to the Throne... but they sure guessed right about the explosion thing, huh?" "Yes, the Tsar would look quite silly if I had actually died from sniper fire," he responded snidely.

She spun around while still pointing at the screen, "Wow, and here is our marriage certificate... I told them about 'us'... you're never getting rid of me now, ha ha!" He laughed, imitating an aristocrat of old, stating, "Woe is me," with obvious sarcasm.

"Hold on, there is more info coming. Wait, what?" she said, looking at the screen in bewilderment, "the Tsar, He, His Highness... has made you acting prince of Titan 'until such time that proper elections can be organized or for a maximum of five years, with no possibility for a second term'... that means..." She leaned out of the ship like an actress in a musical and spread her arms, "... I'm a princess! Princess... Ivanova!"

He raised his head from the ground, put his arm behind his skull, propping it up with his forearm, "With all sincerity, I congratulate you with your stunning achievement. Now could you help me get my gear off and wash the blood off of me?" Her eyes widened, "Oh, right, that, coming, my beloved... Prince of Titan."

[End of Document: The events after this point cannot be revealed to the public or even You, sir. -Signed, Assistant to the Security Council, A. Imashev.]

Evolutionary Strategies

During the time of what would be the second millennia of Holy Rus', especially after the discovery of 3D chemistry and its cataclysmic methodology, the key principle and dividing line between human civilizations no longer remained religious, ideological, or purely geopolitical. It instead became the question of how each given civilization would approach the next phase of human evolution.

These positions possess an ideological component but they are not political per se and do not necessarily reflect any particular political system, even if in one civilization they are directly attached to one another. Two people could believe in the same political theory and yet be opposed in their views on evolutionary strategy and vice versa. The concept of "political realism" has gone nowhere, and remains the dominant and most *istina* interpretation of international relations—states act in their own self interests. But with the human species branching off, that driving force of pragmatism is weaker when dealing with those whom we may consider to be an entirely different species.

The most common evolutionary strategies are the following, listed in order from most human to least human in their nature:

Rejectionism, Naturalism, Original Human Form: A plurality of the sentient life in the solar system remains human as in ancient centuries past. They have no ability or desire to change. Holy Russians refer to these vast and diverse groups as "Southerners."

Cybernetic Utilitarianism: Any embrace of "cybernetics" means that this society accepts that humans can enhance themselves with direct mechanical technology. A utilitarian approach, most associated with China, is the most skeptical position on this issue. This view believes that these enhancements should be strictly controlled by the government and only used when necessary and for a good practical reason. Each cybernetic enhancement should be allocated according to absolute needs and benefit to society and the individual and not for fun, luxury, or some other frivolous emotional purpose.

Cybernetic Humanism: This is the belief that humans should embrace any mechanical upgrades that do not conflict with their ultimate "humanness." This is the position of Holy Rus' and is embodied in the cybernetics of the Ultra Heavies. On the one hand, they possess abilities that would seem god-like in comparison to a normal human, but genetically and psychologically they are still men. They still have a sex drive, normal emotional needs, families, friends, traditions and so on. In fact, in order to anchor these cyborgs to reality, cybernetic humanists place great value in religion, culture and tradition to balance out the individual—keeping them ultimately human.

Cybernetic Libertarianism: This position argues that any cybernetic enhancements should be allowed to anyone who can afford them. It is the belief that there should be no restriction on customization of the individual as he sees fit. This hyper-individualistic approach is not beneficial to empire building and thus this view is restricted to being a popular subculture movement across the solar system, with the exception of the Confederate States of America where these values are enshrined in law.

Mechanical Supremacism: This is the belief that not only is machine superior to man, but that man is best off serving machine in harmony. Certain cultures that faced extreme population decline like Japan turned to robotics more and more to answer all problems in life, till it became clear that it was the human element that was holding the machines down from achieving greater things.

All attempts to produce a sentient AI species have failed. Thus nothing can control robots as well as the human mind, which still retains will and beliefs. Those who live in a mechanical supremacist society are few and generally live completely alone, serviced for their biological needs by primitive robots while they themselves operate advanced ones. This movement is not "popular" in so much as it was a reaction to extreme population decline within at least one major civilization Thus this world view is not discussed or proselytized. This type of society is not only closed off from an individual level but on a societal one, which is reflected in Neo Japan's policy of "total isolation for 5,000 years."

It is important to note that the human part of this type of society are essentially "normal" people in a genetic sense, even if they live their entire lives alone in a box, mostly using VR to interact with the outside world.

Genetic Idealism: This is the belief that through genetic manipulation and organic technology we can elevate man to an angelic god-like pure form. This goal is pursued both positively by constant governmental experimentation and augmentation of the population and negatively via eugenics. This type of society tends to be extremely vicious to those it sees as inferior, which generally includes all of those who are normal humans or possess only cybernetic enhancements. This quest for genetic perfection leaves many victims, but the true believers see this as not only natural but a benefit to such a policy. The Fascists, for example, even see within their own society many "sub-

Aryans" not worthy of life. This desire to create total purity brings this type of society into constant conflict with other evolutionary strategies.

Speciation: Since it has become possible to essentially force human evolution down different paths or rewrite genetics entirely, there are some societies that have chosen to simply become something else and completely non-human. This strategy is present in some pockets of colonized worlds but is only truly seen as a state policy in Greater Rwanda.

Mutation: Unlike other evolutionary strategies, mutation happens seemingly by unknown forces (or the will of Satan) in areas that experienced an extremely concentrated usage of cataclysmic 3D chemistry, especially during terraforming. As Earth was not terraformed, the appearance of mutants there is rare. Furthermore, this process tends to happen nearly instantly in a cataclysmic way, affecting multiple people with the same mutation at once. However, the high spiritual fortitude of an individual can provide resistance to this effect, leading one to believe it is a demonic phenomenon. Mutants are no longer genetically human, and different packs of mutants are not compatible for reproduction.

The only stable and reproducing society of mutants that is known of are the Cherty of Io. However, their natural state of social organization may lead to their own extinction within a few generations. Mutation is a form of speciation. However, it is unplanned and not reflective of any sort of state policy. It is a supernatural non-human phenomenon.

Complete Post-Humanism (AI): All attempts to convert a human mind to AI have failed. All attempts to create some type of android have also failed. There is no example of this evolutionary strategy working successfully.

Timeline of Events

The Great Ages of Holy Rus' Listed by Century AD

The beginning of time till the 10th century: The unknowable and foreign history

10th: Christening of Holy Rus' and the beginning of our history

10th-20th: The millennium of tradition-building

20th-21st: The first crisis of meaninglessness

21st-30th: The millennium of many Tsars

30th-31st: The interplanetary civil-war era and the second crisis of meaninglessness

31st-40th: The millennium of the single Tsar

Dawn of the 40th: The present and the time period of the events of this book—the year 3900 AD.

40th or 41st: The coming great crisis of meaning

Time Unknown: The End of Times and the Apocalypse

Other Important Events

22nd: The discovery of 3D chemistry and later the invention of the converter

23rd: The basics of terraforming prove to be viable

31st: The founding of the Ultra Heavies

List of Inhabited and/or Terraformed Worlds by Holy Rus'

- Mercury (0% control, terraforming failed)

- Venus (5% control of landmass)

- Earth (15% control of landmass)

- The Moon (10% control of landmass, non-terraformed)

- Mars (40% control of landmass)

- Ganymede (60% control of landmass)

- Callisto (30% control of landmass)

- Io (60% control of landmass)

- Europa (50% control of landmass)

- Titan (one colony attempted, status unclear, no competitors present)

Glossary

Civilian Rifle – The most common weapon in Holy Rus', given from father to son upon completion of the rites of manhood. It is a rifle based on the ancient but reliable AK platform, firing semi-auto with ten-round magazines.

Converter: A mechanism that allows for "cataclysmic 3D chemical reactions" to take place in a controlled manner. It can be used to deconstruct and separate materials or "convert" them into other like materials. For example, most bio matter can be converted into gasoline or other hydrocarbons.

Curse of Terraforming (The Curse): The effect that large amounts of "cataclysmic 3D chemical reactions" have on the human body, resulting in people being turned into mutants and abominations. This is the price of terraforming other worlds.

Domain: The territory that an Ultra Heavy or other person of high status has control over. They, to some extent, govern the lives and activities happening on this land as an overseer and sheriff.

Gauntlet: Heavy arm protection that also provides ID, banking, and other digital services/functions. Gauntlets are powered by an internal converter

Hauberk: The massive set of armor that many of the Ultra Heavies wear. It is made up of an extreme thick "coat of plates," which is pocketed to accept *troika* steel plates in an organized way. These suits of armor have an enormous amount of optional features too long to list.

Helm: Protective headgear with computerized elements powered from an internal converter. It provides "omnipresent" vision on all sorts of spectrums and in every direction. It links to the user's brain directly via a port installed on the neck of the wearer.

Holy Rus': How Russians refer to Russia formally in the year 3900 AD. Russians themselves are officially "Holy Russians" on documentation for the sake of consistency.

Internal Converter: This is a converter that works inside of the human body, converting fat and nutrients to real world electrical energy. It is a miniature power plant in a way. Users of this device tend to have bodies that look like Greek statues as all fat is being burned while their muscles are constantly stimulated.

***Istina* (*Istinoo*):** The actual deeper factual or objective truth of something. Water is made of hydrogen and oxygen is *istina*.

Katechon: A theological and religious-political concept based on Christian eschatology. It is a historical entity, usually a state, with a mission to prevent the final triumph of evil in history, the arrival of the Antichrist and delay the end of the world. It is popular among Orthodox monarchists to identify with the "detaining" Orthodox Tsar.

Long Night: The night on Titan lasts over two weeks in terms of Earth days. This has a major effect on the way people live on Titan.

Nanorestoration, Nanomachines, Nanohealing: Extremely complex networks of microscopic or nearly microscopic machines that can restore and heal nearly any wounds suffered by the user. Because of this technology, there are virtually no disabled individuals except for the extremely elderly in Holy Rus'.

***Pravda* (*Pravdoo*):** The political or subjective truth of something. If someone says they love when it rains water from the sky, this is *pravda*.

Prime Directive: The only clear purpose for human existence carried down by the Church and presented to man from God in the Bible is that we as humans must "go forth and multiply." That is, we must survive. Thus the primary function of Holy Rus' is to continue the survival of its own Russian civilization, including the nationalities that share its historical destiny, through *"fighting, fucking, fraternity or whatever works, so long as we never abandon our humanity."*

Throne, The: This refers to the entire administration that works directly for the Tsar, numbering about 10,000 people who deal with all of his affairs. This includes the Inner and Outer Guard, secretaries, organizers, bureaucrats, lawyers and cheerleaders.